CW00855054

Facing the ~~Dark~~

Everything had changed the moment I opened the door to the two men. It was worse, somehow, that I had been the one to let them in, the one who ended our family life.

Simon's father has been accused of the murder of a rival cab driver and Simon faces a life branded as the son of a murderer. Then he meets Charley, grieving for her dead father, the murder victim, and they determine to find out the real story behind the murder. Together they can face up to the danger which surrounds them, and bring back some hope for the future.

MICHAEL HARRISON was born in Oxford in 1939. He has taught in North Queensland, London, Oxford, and Hartlepool but is now retired and enjoys visiting schools as a writer. He is married and has two grown-up sons. His previous books include a history of witches, funny novels, retellings of Norse myths, a book of poems, *Junk Mail*, a retelling of *Don Quixote*, and *It's My Life*, his first novel for Oxford University Press.

Facing the Dark

Other Oxford fiction

Facing the Dark

Michael Harrison

OXFORD
UNIVERSITY PRESS

OXFORD
UNIVERSITY PRESS

Great Clarendon Street, Oxford OX2 6DP

Oxford University Press is a department of the University of Oxford.
It furthers the University's objective of excellence in research, scholarship,
and education by publishing worldwide in

Oxford New York

Athens Auckland Bangkok Bogotá Buenos Aires Calcutta
Cape Town Chennai Dar es Salaam Delhi Florence Hong Kong Istanbul
Karachi Kuala Lumpur Madrid Melbourne Mexico City Mumbai
Nairobi Paris São Paulo Singapore Taipei Tokyo Toronto Warsaw

and associated companies in Berlin Ibadan

British Library Cataloguing in Publication Data available

Cover illustration by Paul Young

ISBN 0 19 275053 4

Typeset by AFS Image Setters Ltd, Glasgow

Printed and bound in Great Britain by
Cox & Wyman Ltd

1
Simon

Dad was arrested for murder on Tuesday. When the
door closed behind the police Mum and I just sat on the
sofa and stared at the floor for what seemed a very long
time. Then she went out across the hall to the kitchen
and I heard her filling the kettle. She brought me a mug
of very sweet tea and told me to drink it. She sounded
strange, as if she was a very long way away, or perhaps I
was. Everything had changed the moment I opened the
door to the two men. It was worse, somehow, that I had
been the one to let them in, the one who ended our
family life.

It had been very quick: Is your father in? I'm
Inspector Something and this is Sergeant Something
Else. Could we have a word with him, please? And then
reciting his rights to him, so familiar from watching *The
Bill*. And they were gone and we were left.

'What's he done?' I said, staring into my mug of tea.

'Nothing,' Mum said. 'It's a mistake, you'll see.'

My mind wouldn't leave that moment when I opened
the door. I kept thinking I should have slammed it shut,
or said he wasn't there, or . . . Two men, ordinary men
in suits.

And then the word 'murder' leapt out of the words of
the caution—I am arresting you for the murder of—and
I shook so hard the tea slopped out of my mug on to my
jeans.

'They said "murder". . . '

'Your dad wouldn't murder anyone,' Mum said. 'Not
actual murder.'

'But who?'

'Oh God, no!' Mum moaned. She got up and went

1

out into the kitchen again. I suddenly knew what she was doing. She was rummaging through the pile of old newspapers in the cupboard under the sink. She used to throw the paper in there every evening saying that she hadn't had time to read it, she was too busy. When the cupboard was so full the door wouldn't shut she'd get them all out and go through them, clucking and tutting over news that was weeks or months old. Then Dad had to take the great heap round to the waste-paper skip and it would all start up again.

The rustling stopped and there was silence. I stood up, easing my tea-soaked jeans off my thighs. I walked, forced myself to walk, into the kitchen. Mum's tall, with long fair hair; elegant, Dad used to call her. She is also full of life, bursting with energy and enthusiasm— usually.

Now she was very still, bent over. She had last week's local newspaper spread on the table. I stood next to her. It was the main story on the front page. The headline lay there like letters carved into a tombstone:

ROAD RAGE KILLING?

There was a large smudgy photograph of a car, a Ford Granada, and an inset of a smiling, bald-headed man.

Mum saw me looking and turned the paper over.

3 NIL DOWN!

shouted up now instead. Dad, Mum, me. Three of us. Down.

'You'll be late for school,' Mum said without looking at me.

I stared at her. School? How could I go to school

when my father had just been arrested for murder? Walk in to . . . what? Silence and turned backs? Shouts and jeers? Embarrassed sympathy? Questions and questions and questions to which I had no answers at all.

'No one's going to know today,' Mum said, reading my mind, 'and tomorrow it'll all be over. Anyway, I've got a lot of things I must do, solicitor, that sort of thing. I don't want you on your own, worrying. Get to school and get your mind off everything. I'll be here when you get back, and Dad too, you'll see.'

There was no way I was going to school but I didn't want to row with Mum about it. I shrugged my shoulders, went out into the hall and picked up my school bag. Mum came after me. I could see she was all ready for an emotional farewell but I couldn't cope with that so I just turned, threw a goodbye over my shoulder, and opened the door for the second time that morning. When one door shuts, they all shut, I thought, looking at all the closed front-doors across the road. Nothing was making sense this morning, especially not my thoughts.

As I walked down the path towards the gate the doors disappeared behind the snarling traffic and just the upper windows glared at me, disapprovingly. I turned right towards school in case Mum was watching and walked until I was out of sight round the corner.

There perhaps was part of the answer to my immediate problem: Blandy's Stores, a grand name for a run-down newsagents, tobacconist, and sweet shop. Mr Blandy was resting his pot-belly on the counter as usual, the usual cigarette ash down his green cardigan. He grunted when I went in. He hated school kids, perhaps especially as we were about the only people who used his shop. I couldn't see the local paper with the few dailies he had laid out in front of him. Somehow I couldn't bring myself to ask. I thought if I did he would know why I wanted it. I couldn't bear the thought of him knowing. I bought a bar of chocolate, putting the

3

right change down on the counter. Mr Blandy grunted again and I went out.

I wasn't going to school. Where was I going? I needed to read the newspaper. The proper newsagents in the town centre would have it, and it was in the opposite direction from school. That would be my best bet. I stood on the side of the road, waiting for a chance to cross. The traffic was moving just enough to make it difficult, one car after another, grinding in bottom gear, trailing exhaust stink behind. I gave up and walked along, aiming for the lights. It took me out of my way a bit, but I wasn't really in any hurry. I had the day to fill, somehow. At least it had stopped raining today.

As I got nearer to the centre of town I remembered the library. They would have the local paper. They'd have a quiet place I could sit and read it, and think, and if anyone asked why I wasn't in school I could say I was doing a project. Which was the truth, really, only it wasn't a project for school.

The library was up three stone steps and through two pairs of swing doors and was just opening. A couple of old women with shopping bags were clucking in. The noise of the traffic was hushed by the first pair, cut out by the second. Across the room the headline shouted at me from the periodicals rack. I walked towards it, starting to tremble again.

'Can I help you?' the librarian asked as I passed her desk. Unlike Mr Blandy she smiled, and was smartly dressed.

'The local paper, for a project,' I said. She smiled and pointed at it.

'Just say if you want any help.' If only it was that easy!

I took the paper to an empty table and laid it out. I swallowed hard, held on to the chair to stop my shaking, and started to read.

4

ROAD RAGE KILLING?

THE BODY of local businessman Bill Westcot was found on Wednesday night in his burnt-out car on the Thorney to Grafton road. He had suffered head injuries. Inspector Mopper who is in charge of the investigation said that the police were keeping an open mind. He agreed that this could be another 'road rage' killing. 'It is much too early to say,' he cautioned. 'This could just be a tragic accident.' He is keen for any possible witnesses to come forward and would like to hear from anyone who used the Grafton to Thorney road between 6 p.m. and 1 a.m. on Wednesday.

Bill Westcot, of 16 Chidham Road, was well-known in the local community, not only as the owner of Westcot Cabs but for his charity work for disabled children. His wife, Christine, was too shocked to speak yesterday but Mr Westcot's brother, Henry Westcot, urged anyone with information to talk to the police. Bill Westcot leaves a widow and a daughter.

I read this several times and then sat and stared at it. William Westcot had been the name the police used when they arrested Dad. It hadn't meant anything to me at the time but now it rang inside my head: William Westcot, William Westcot, William Westcot . . .

I rummaged in my school bag and then remembered. In my hurry to leave the house I had left my pencil case upstairs with my homework. I went over to the librarian. She looked up from her computer and smiled. The library was so quiet it was difficult to break the silence. 'I'm sorry,' I said. 'I left my bag behind.' Before I could finish she passed me a pencil and a sheet of computer print-out.

'Anything else?'

'Is there a local Ordnance Survey map?' She pointed to the shelves to the left of the newspapers with a label: 'Local Reference'. 'Thanks!' I said. 'I'll bring the pencil back.'

'You do that,' she said. 'I don't want to have to get the police after you.'

Very funny, I thought as I walked back, and was glad I hadn't gone to school. I found the map and took it to my table. I didn't know why I was doing this. I hadn't yet had my Great Idea so I suppose I was partly just filling in time, giving myself something to do so I didn't have to leave the safety of the library. I have to admit, too, that part of me believed Dad must be guilty or he wouldn't have been arrested. And there were other things that I tried to push away, out of my mind, which kept trying to come back when I wasn't looking: nagging thoughts . . .

I found Grafton. It was about five miles north-east of our house. Thorney was another four miles or so further on along a B road. I tried to trace the map but the piece of paper she'd given me was too opaque to see through and the print on the back ghosted through in places. I turned it over. It was part of the library catalogue, a list of authors and books and numbers and symbols and little letters.

Christie, Agatha: Murder on the Nile

caught my eye, perhaps because there'd been yet another repeat of it on TV last week. It was then I got my Great Idea. I couldn't really kid myself I could solve the crime like Hercule Poirot, but becoming a private investigator would give me something to do, somewhere to go, an escape from my thoughts. It was better than sitting around.

I turned the paper over and made a careful copy of the map, showing the route from our house. I wrote down the details from the newspaper account: names, addresses, times. I found a local street plan on the bookshelf and drew a plan to show where Chidham Road was and then found Westcot Cabs in *Yellow Pages*, and where they were. I added our house to this plan.

I thought I'd probably spent as much time as I could without attracting suspicion so I put the piece of paper in my pocket, returned the maps to the shelf and took the pencil back to the librarian.

'Did you find what you wanted?'

'Yes, thank you very much. But I may have to come again to check some things.'

'That's what we're here for,' she said.

It was difficult walking out of the library. The traffic roared at me as if it was hungry beasts desperate to tear me to pieces. I shrugged and hurried home. I needed my bike.

2
Simon

I cycled out of town towards Grafton. It was a beautiful spring morning. I was buoyed up for the moment by the fantasy that I was going to find some vital piece of evidence the plodding police had missed and set my father free. I composed newspaper articles in my head as I rode along, each more effusive than the last. I forgot that you must never hope too much.

I was brought back to my senses by the blare of a car's horn, a black BMW, as it zoomed past me. I made a rude sign after it. The car screeched to a halt down the road and a red-faced man erupted out of it, shouting and swearing as he came:

'Why the ✳✳✳✳ aren't you in school instead of swerving all over the ✳✳✳✳ing road?' He took a mobile phone out of his pocket and waved it at me like a weapon. 'I've a good mind to ring the police and report you. In fact I will ring your school and report you for truancy. What school do you go to? Eh?'

'Henry Harting,' I lied. That was the other school in the town. Somehow I wasn't frightened of this man. I should have been, and it frightened me later when I thought about it. I was alone on a country road with an angry stranger. No one knew where I was. He could have done anything he wanted. Somehow I just saw him as pathetic: a little red-faced man jumping up and down and using naughty words to a kid on a bike. He waved his phone at me once more.

'I really haven't got the time to bother,' he said. 'If you want to waste your opportunities of a good education and get yourself killed in the process, well, good luck to you.' He strode back to his car and spurted off down the road with a squeal of rubber. I waved, politely, after him, once he was round the next bend. The smell of his exhaust hung in the air.

As I cycled along my mind made up new newspaper reports, against my will, reports of my body found dumped in a ditch:

> ' . . . it looks as if he had been bludgeoned to death with a mobile phone,' said Inspector MopSomething. 'There's no apparent motive and we don't know why he was there. His mother, who is naturally distraught, said she thought he had gone to school . . . '

Grafton had a village shop. I hesitated over going in but I was beginning to feel really hungry, and craving more chocolate. There were three women in the shop, two customers and the shop woman behind the counter and they all stared at me. 'No school?' one of them said, a bit nastily.

'Teachers have got one of their study days,' I said. 'School's closed.' I thought they all looked too old to have children at school still. I knew Grafton kids got bused in to our school.

'I don't know why they can't study in their holidays,' the other customer said, 'they get enough.'

'I wanted to look at the church,' I said, throwing it to them like meat to a guard dog. 'Do you know if it's open?'

As I cycled away I wondered what would have happened if I'd told them the truth. I don't think they would have been as friendly as they turned out, wouldn't have been friendly at all. I wondered if I would ever be able to tell the truth again. Fortunately the church was the way I needed to go anyway, and round a corner so it looked as if I was going that way.

I had thought I was going to cycle straight past but when I turned the corner and saw the great stone building towering over its graveyard I found I was braking and turning towards the gate. I knew as I walked between the rows of gravestones that I was just being superstitious but somehow its being a church made it worse. At the back of my mind thunderbolts hovered. I was afraid of what Fate, or God, might do next if I tempted It, or Him. I had said I was going to visit the church, so that was what I was going to do. Anyway, I was in no hurry.

I didn't spend much time there. I walked round, not knowing what I was looking at. We had never been a church-going, or church-visiting, family so I had no idea what you did. I sat down for a moment at the back and thought, Let it be all right, which was the nearest I could get to praying, and then a girl of about my age came in and walked hurriedly up to the front pew and knelt down. I wondered briefly what she was doing out of school and left as quietly as I could.

I cycled along the quiet country road, past hawthorn hedges and grassy verges. It was all so green and fresh after all the rain we'd had. There were so few cars that each one was a separate noise coming and going, a separate smell. The sun was shining, the birds were singing, the flowers were blooming: it certainly beat school.

And then I came round a sharp corner and braked hard. I put my bike down carefully on the verge and stood and looked. It was so obvious that it was the right place. I wished I'd brought my camera, or a notebook and pencil. Perhaps I should go and fetch them and come back. Perhaps the scene would burn itself into my memory. Perhaps I didn't want it to lodge itself there?

The first impression was of blackness. The grass was

scorched, withered. The hedge turned wintry with curled, dried leaves. Flakes of ash drifted slightly. You might have thought there had been a large bonfire there, or that a flying saucer had landed briefly. It's a black hole, a black hole, I kept saying to myself. In the middle of the green fields and hedges with the last of the creamy May blossom and roadside flowers was blackness, deadness. My normal life had been burnt up here, never to be the same again. I didn't believe Dad could have done this, but I knew that innocent people had been convicted and had spent years in prison before being let out. Some, surely, were innocent and were never let out?

I feel ashamed of myself, but I worried about my life as the son of a convicted murderer. Scenes from the future crowded in and wouldn't go away.

The verge itself had been cut up, ploughed up, so that brown earth showed like miniature empty graves. The hedge beyond had been savaged: branches ripped off leaving long white scars visible in places under the blackness. Violence had been done here.

On the other side of the road was a large notice on a two-sided stand:

HELP NEEDED!

Were you on this road
last Wednesday, May 7th,
between 6 p.m. and 1 a.m.?
If you were, please
ring the police
on 01865-52371.

I walked slowly along the road. There was a scrap of blue and white plastic tape with POLICE on it still in the hedge. They must have finished their searches, photographed everything, collected anything there was to collect. How stupid I was to think that the Great Boy Detective could cycle out and find the vital piece of evidence that had eluded the simple-minded country plods and free his father with one brilliant stroke. I felt tears pricking my eyes and blinked angrily. Great Boy Detectives don't cry.

I stood and stared down at the torn-up verge, at the blackness. I had seen enough. I had looked into the future and seen nothing but pain and emptiness and despair. I turned and walked slowly back to my bike. The bright morning mocked me now. I walked in my own night.

It was this very hopelessness that gave me my first real glimmer of hope. I was cycling very slowly home, each pedal stroke an individual effort, making the gentle hill seem a Sisyphean mountain, my head down, not really looking where I was going. I was some metres past before I realized what I had seen. I got off, laid my bike down again, and walked back.

Cutting into the verge. Tyre tracks. Like the other ones. Identical? I didn't know. I hadn't noticed them coming. I suppose there was no reason I should. You might well not notice them at all if you were driving along in a car, thinking about where you were going, or what you had come from. They must have been at least a mile from where the car had been burnt. They looked the same but thousands of cars must have the same tyres. I cursed myself again for not bringing my camera, for not buying a pencil in the shop.

I walked up and down, crouched, stood. I have to admit I had no real idea what I was doing, or why. The GBD would have done a Sherlock Holmes: 'These marks must have been done when the ground was soft.

12

We had ninety-seven millimetres of rain between 4 p.m. and 6 p.m. on . . . Therefore they were made by a red-haired man wearing jeans. His mother once went to Blackpool . . . '

I heard the squeal of bicycle brakes and looked round. The girl from the church was about five metres away, astride her bike, staring at me.

'What are you doing?'

She got off and pushed her bike towards me. She was a bit shorter than me, round faced, brown hair to her shoulders, almost tubby. She ought to be the standard smiling easy-going type but as she came closer I could see she had great black bags under her eyes and her face was very drawn and unhappy. I remembered how she had walked into the church and dropped to her knees to pray.

'What are you doing?' she said again and I realized I had been staring at her.

'Looking at these tyre marks. It looks as though a car's come off the road here. I was wondering what had happened.'

'If you're one of those ghouls looking for the murder scene you're in the wrong place,' she said angrily. She got back on her bike and cycled quickly away.

'I'm not!' I called after her, and noticed the bunch of flowers wrapped in paper in her rear basket, and suddenly realized who she was.

And I suddenly realized too that this wasn't just my tragedy. It was spreading into life after life.

I stared after her until she went round the corner. Somehow I was jealous of her. She could grieve, and everyone would be sorry for her. How would people treat me?

I ought to tell her I was sorry, sorry her father was dead, but she must believe that mine had killed him. She must hate me. I hated myself. I turned back and looked down at the ground again, at the tyre marks.

13

I stared at them. Were they the same? If they were the same, why had the car gone on to the verge twice? That didn't make sense. It was most likely nothing to do with Dad's case, but I suddenly found I just had to know. I must find out everything I could.

3
Charley

It's what I hate most. Nosy people, ghouls. All the
varieties of nosy people. And by now I'm an expert,
could write a guide: *The Ghoul: A Field Guide* by
Charlotte Westcot. We've done all that stuff on making
a Key in biology, how you look for the distinguishing
feature, and we've done a practice one on our class. How
Chloe's Doc Martins wouldn't do because she only wore
them on days when we didn't have Mrs Batlow who was
fanatical about The School Dress Policy, as she called it.
Emily suggested using her sulky expression but Amy
claimed she'd seen her smile once last September so that
wasn't any good either . . .

As I cycle I make it up in my head. I make a lot of
things up in my head these days. It stops me
remembering.

The Ghoul: A Field Guide by Charlotte Westcot
    1. Does it carry a camera or a notebook?
      If camera, it's a tabloid photographer
      If notebook, it's a tabloid reporter
        If neither, go to 2.
    2. Did you know the Ghoul in your previous life?
      If no, it might be a reporter in disguise
        If yes, it's—

It's almost worse. If Dad had just died all the
sympathy that's been poured over me like custard over
a stodgy pudding might perhaps be sweet and warm and
comforting. But he didn't just die and there's that
ghoulish craving for the gory details under the
sympathy. Mum doesn't seem to see it. She sits there,

knee-deep in custard, surrounded by Ghouls, going over and over everything the police have told her until I'm at screaming point and have to get out of the house, even though I'll probably meet Ghouls hanging about. I've given up coming in the front gate but now I leave my bike locked to the lamp-post in the snicket and climb over the back fence.

It gives me a shock, seeing that boy standing there by the side of the road. I'm so surprised—why isn't he in school?—that I brake hard and look at him. He has his back to me and is crouched over the verge.

'What are you doing?' I say. He twists round and then stands up. He doesn't look like a ghoul. He looks about my age, tall and skinny, fair-haired. He stares at me. I notice he holds his shoulders up, as if frozen in a shrug. It gives him a tense look.

'What are you doing?' I repeat.

'Looking at the tyre marks.' He points at the verge and I see brown smears on the grass. 'It looks as though a car's come off here. I was wondering about it.'

I snap, 'If you're looking for the murder scene you're in the wrong place.' I stand on the pedals and ride quickly away. He shouts something after me but I just keep going. Tears come to my eyes again.

Why isn't he in school? I wonder. Then I'm where it happened and I get slowly off my bike and lower it to the ground. Grass comes through the spokes as if it's trying to suck it down. I take the bunch of flowers out of the carrier and walk towards the marks. I guess where the car was by the marks: tyre marks leading into the verge and then stopping suddenly, finally. I put the flowers down where I think the front seat would be. They make the blackened ground still more desolate: a spilt brightness. I don't cry now. I feel numbness on this spot where my father's life ended, where my being his child ended.

It's as though the lighthouse beam has suddenly been

switched off and I'm at sea in the dark, the unseen waves arching over me. All my life I have been the centre of my parents' regard, and now my father's light has gone out and Mum's has dimmed so that she hardly seems to be there at all. A shadow has replaced her. 'The breath of the night wind'—we read that in a poem last week. I can feel that breath now.

I'm aware suddenly that the boy is standing watching me again. A ghoul of the worst kind: sucking up my misery, thirsting for my tears. I try ignoring him first, hoping he'll get embarrassed or bored and just go away. But he doesn't. He stands there, itching in the corner of my eye so that I want to rub it to remove him. From there his presence swells till it fills my mind and I can't think of Dad at all. The bunch of flowers I picked from the garden, the flowers he grew so carefully, lie wrapped in their paper looking pathetic. The black grass is a better memorial for him. If the boy hadn't been watching me I'd have picked them up and taken them home again.

'I'm sorry about your father,' he says suddenly. I don't bother to answer. So many people have said that these nightmare days; it's become a meaningless mantra. This time it just irritates me. 'Sorry,' he says. Sorry is what we say when we're apologizing, when it's our fault. What's Dad's death to do with him?

He comes forward slowly, hesitantly. I cringe. Is he going to put his arms round me? Lots of people have done that, too, and it doesn't help. It's only Dad's arms I want. I get quite angry. I certainly don't want some boy taking advantage of the situation to get his hands on me. He stops about a metre away and drops to his knees as if he's going to pray. That doesn't work either, I could tell him. I tried, and it doesn't work. But I don't say anything at all.

He bends forward and stares at the ground. He puts out his fingers and gently touches the tyre marks, gently traces their pattern. I suddenly want to stretch my hand out and touch his head, his soft fair hair, but I don't. I hold myself rigid.

'They're not the same,' he says in a surprised voice. He turns then and looks me in the face. Blue eyes stare up at me, puzzled. 'They're not the same tyres,' he says again. 'A different car made these marks.' I think, So what? He goes on, as if I'd spoken, or as if he doesn't expect me to speak. 'They look the same age. It would be strange: two different cars violently off the road this distance apart, at about the same time.' He sits back on his heels and goes on looking at me.

'I'm sorry,' he says after a pause. 'You must think me insensitive. Perhaps it doesn't matter to you, but it does to me, it really does. I need to know.'

He stands up and walks away, back to his bike. I stare at him. He looks tense and dejected. Who is he? I leave the flowers and cycle slowly home, and wish I hadn't.

'Uncle John' is there. I know why he's there and I hate him for it and I hate the way he calls himself Uncle John. I don't call him anything, not out loud. To myself I call him Short John, though he's not a pirate and he hasn't got a wooden leg or a parrot. But he is short and I don't trust him an inch, the slimy short sod. He's not a ghoul exactly, more of a vulture, come to feed off the carcass.

They're in the kitchen, either side of the table, coffee mugs in front of them. Mum looks up as I come in and smiles, wetly. Short John jumps up, at least as far up as he can get. I'm looking forward to the time when I'm actually taller than him. I promise myself I'll pat him on the head then, and remember the boy and how my hand nearly went out to his head and feel embarrassed. I feel embarrassed walking in anyway.

Short John rushes over and clasps my hand in both of his. I'm sure he'd kiss me if he dared but I hold myself so he can't. This is bad enough. He puts this soppy expression on his face. 'Charlotte! How *are* you?'

I take my hand away and go and sit next to Mum. He's around too much. I thought at first he was after Mum but she's told me he's made an offer for the business. She told me at breakfast. I think that's why I went out with the flowers, I was so angry. We haven't even had the funeral yet and he's there with his great slobbery lips picking away.

'It's a fair offer,' Mum said, 'and it'll be a big weight off my shoulders.'

'Dad would want you to carry on,' I said, amazed that she could even think of selling, amazed at his cheek in trying to buy it before Dad was even in the ground. What would Mum do, I wondered, without the business to run? Dad always said she did all the hard work: the phone, the books.

'But if I do, and it doesn't work out . . . I'm not sure I can face it . . . '

'What about Amit?' I said. Amit drives for Dad. Amit is Amy's father. Amy is my best friend. My best friend's father out of a job. 'And it's too soon,' I said.

'He needs an answer soon, he says. Business reasons he didn't want to bother me with . . . '

Vulture, I say to him in my mind as he sits at the table again.

> Vulture vulgaris: related to the Greedy
> Ghoul. Often appears as John Hunston,
> aka 'Uncle John', owner of Caring Cars,
> the biggest taxi firm in the district, and
> hire cars, and self-drive, and funeral
> directors . . .

'Where did you go, love?' Mum asks, but she asks as if she's not really interested, as if she isn't inside her body any longer, her comfortable familiar mumness.

'I went to where Dad died,' I say. I want to remind Short John that we're thinking about Dad, not about his business. Mum puts her hand on mine and squeezes it.

'Was that a good idea, Charlotte?' Short John asks.

I know Mum thinks I'm unfair about him. 'He's been kind and thoughtful,' she keeps saying, 'and so practical. I don't really know what I would have done without him.' So I bite back what I would really like to say, for her sake.

'There was a boy there,' I say, knowing I have to say something and thinking of her, knowing she needs to talk about Dad all the time, over and over. 'He was looking at the tyre marks. He said there was something odd about them.'

'What sort of boy?' Short John asks. Mum squeezes my hand again. I go on talking. It's so embarrassing, sitting here at the kitchen table with Short John in Dad's chair looking all concerned and smarmy and phony and Mum all weepy and me wanting to be weepy, but not in front of him. I make a story out of it, as if it was some spooky thriller on TV. Mum just sits and holds my hand but Short John enters into the spirit of it and asks questions about the boy to keep it all going.

In the end even he seems bored by the whole thing and gets up and kisses Mum and urges her to think carefully about what he's offering, it's in her best interests, etc, etc . . . I keep well away from him and let Mum see him out. I pick up his mug and wash it very, very thoroughly and then just stare out of the kitchen window. How am I going to get through the rest of today?

4
Simon

I watched the girl cycle back along the road and round the corner. Perhaps I should have told her who I was, but she'd surely already have believed the story that Dad had killed her father so at best she'd have been rude to me, perhaps screamed hysterically. I looked down at the bunch of flowers lying on the blackened and torn-up ground. They too would be dead soon but the grass would recover, would heal over the damaged places, the tyre tracks.

I was sure the tread pattern was different, and I was sure that fact was important, though I couldn't think why. I cursed myself yet again for not bringing my camera. I thought of going home to fetch it but knew that when I got back into the safety of home I wouldn't want to come out again, especially as it would be around out-of-school time. I could not face even my friends, and there were some at school who would seize upon Dad's arrest and hound me viciously.

A notebook, though, I could surely buy at the village shop. I could draw the patterns and perhaps come out tomorrow with my camera. I certainly wasn't going to school. If Mum turned me out of the house again I'd need something to do.

The shop was empty this time. The shopkeeper came through from the back as the doorbell pinged. She seemed almost pleased to see me. 'You're having a thorough look, I will say.'

It took me a moment to remember that I was supposed to be studying the church. 'I need another notebook,' I said. 'And my pencil broke.' She pointed to a stand in the corner which had a small selection of stationery. I chose a cheap writing pad and a pencil. I checked my money. I had enough for a drink and another chocolate bar as well, but that was all. I would have to survive until I got home. I couldn't eat anything for breakfast this morning but now I was suddenly very hungry. The chocolate helped, but it wouldn't last long. Superstition made me stop at the church again and I had my unsatisfactory picnic leaning against a gravestone that had a stone slab along the ground. The grass was too wet to sit on and I was tired. It was warm in the sun and I dozed off for a few minutes but jolted myself awake when the nightmares started.

I braked instinctively as soon as I saw the black BMW parked by the side of the road. It was about where the first set of tyre marks had been made. There was no way I was going to cycle up and start drawing. It could be anyone. It could be the police. It could be the real murderer. It could be the same car I'd had trouble with already.

There was a gateway on the right that led into a field and I thought of going into there but a few metres back I had passed one of those little green signposts that mark footpaths and bridleways. I pushed my bike through the gap in the hedge and left it pointing away from the road. I could escape from a car down there if I had to, and perhaps from men chasing on foot, if I got a good enough start. The path here looked dry enough for my mountain bike. Perhaps I should have just ridden away then, but I had to know.

The car's engine started up. I walked to the hedge and looked round. The car reversed up the road towards me and then went forward on to the verge and went backwards and forwards several times over the grass, the wheels spinning slightly. It pulled forward on to the road again and the driver got out. It was the same short and angry man in a suit who had shouted at me earlier. He walked along the verge, bent right over, looking intently. He turned, opened the boot of his car and took something out and started scraping at the ground.

I edged forwards to see what he was doing, though I knew really. The only thing he could be doing was erasing the tyre tracks. And if he was, then I had been right and they were important evidence. If I'd had my camera earlier it wouldn't matter so much, or if I had got there in time to draw them . . . But if I'd been earlier he might have seen what I was doing and . . . And what? Driven straight at me? I flinched at the thought and my movement must have caught in the corner of his eye because he stood up and stared straight at me. I froze for a moment and then he stepped towards me and shouted: 'You! Come here!'

I turned at that and ran through the hedge gap and grabbed my bike and jolted uncertainly along the path. As I gained speed the bike wobbled less and I dared a quick look over my shoulder. The man was standing in the gap holding up some metal tool, a tyre lever I guessed. As I turned my head he shouted again but I knew I was safe from him.

The path climbed steadily and twisted round and became more overgrown and muddier. I got off at a steep bit and stood panting, looking back. I was high enough here to be able to see down to the road. The man's car was straight below me. He was leaning against it and seemed to have something spread on the roof that he was studying. A map, I realized. The map I had used myself in the library that morning, so long ago it seemed now. The map that marked footpaths and bridleways. He was seeing where I would come out and he would be there, waiting. Why? He didn't know what I knew but he must be really edgy if he was that worried about me. Perhaps I was just being paranoid and he wasn't interested in me at all.

I sat down so that he wouldn't see me watching him. What was best to do? The trouble was, I just didn't know whether he shouted at any kid he saw or whether he was seriously after me. Pascal's Wager, Dad always said. If you're not sure, what would give the worst result if you're wrong? It was better to guess he was after me and waste effort and time now and be safe. So, wait until he drove off and go back the way I came? He might expect me to do that and could hide round any corner. Once I was back on the road I would be very vulnerable. Go on and hope there were some junctions, alternative paths. I didn't have a map and had no idea where I was headed but at the moment I was relatively high up and so had the advantage of him. If I could get home unseen I should be all right because he could have no idea who I was.

I watched until his car was out of sight and then cycled slowly on. The bridleway had almost levelled out here and ran between tall hedges which seemed to cut out all sounds. The scent of the hawthorn blossom was overwhelming. It would have been a wonderful place to ride for pleasure. Then I was at the top. The ground dropped down on all sides and I was very pleased to see I had come to a crossroads. I had to choose, without a map to help me.

I turned left. This ought to take me more in the direction I wanted to go to get home, and it looked as though it led to a group of farm buildings at the bottom of the hill. There should be a better track from them to a road. I ought to be getting home soon in case Mum was there and started worrying about where I was. If she thought I was going to school like a good boy I'd have several days in which I could . . . Could what? There didn't seem to be anything I could do, but there was no way I was going to school.

I bumped down the track and concentrated on the ground. This was a footpath and quite overgrown. Several times I had to get off and push. There was a hedge on my left and a field of what was probably wheat

24

on my right. Long grass and thistles grew on the path and soon the bottoms of my jeans were soaking wet and clinging to my legs. There was a stile between two fields I had to lift my bike over. I was beginning to get tired and fed up. I wanted to be at home, be dry, have something to eat.

I came at last to the farm buildings I had seen from the top. They looked rather ruined and unused closer up. Any thought I'd had lurking in the back of my mind of knocking at a farmhouse door and a rosy-cheeked farmer's wife giving me a fat slice of cake and a mug of milk fresh from the cow faded back into the Enid Blytons I'd read as a little kid. About the only thing here was nettles, and the heaps of discarded machinery you always see lying around on farms and some straw bales in one of the barns.

Except . . .

There was a car exactly like Dad's taxi in one of the barns. It was right at the back and if my mind hadn't been full of Dad and the police, and perhaps of the Enid Blytons with their easy finding of vital clues in ruined farmyards I might well not have found it at all, but the sun had caught the glass of the back window and flashed at me as I went past. I leant my bike against the wall and went to have a closer look. I suppose it was a way of delaying cycling out and finding a man in a black BMW waiting for me.

Same model. Same colour. Same number plates. Same number plates! I thought for a moment that it was Dad's car, but the police had taken that away this morning on a low-loader. This wasn't exactly a police pound. So what was this? Was I hallucinating through hunger? I went back and hid my bike in another of the buildings, just in case.

As soon as I looked in the car I knew what I had really known all along. It wasn't Dad's. The seats weren't the same colour to start with. There wasn't the machine that priced the journeys. There wasn't Dad's tin of sweets under the dash.

There was an enormous dent in the back door on the driver's side. It looked new because bits of paint were sticking up. Something had hit this car hard. Then I noticed the front door. I must have seen it before but not taken it in: the interlaced TT logo for Tony's Taxis. I crouched down and looked closely at it. It was about the same size and shape; about but not exactly, I thought, but it was much more crudely painted. It might fool you in a bad light but not if you looked carefully.

I walked warily away. I needed to get home, safely. I had to come back, with my camera, before this evidence disappeared too.

5
Charley

Mum's saying goodbye to Short John and suddenly her voice changes. 'Henry!' she cries and I know she's really glad to see him. Dad's brother. No 'uncle' nonsense about him; he's always been just Henry. The trouble is, he's so like Dad I can't bear it. He does a bit of driving for Dad sometimes to help out at weekends and evenings and I keep finding myself wishing it had been him driving on Wednesday and then hating myself because he's always been good to me. But he's not Dad.

I go up the stairs towards my room. I don't want to stay in the kitchen. Mum's at her worst when Henry's here and I can't take it. I don't want to shut myself in my room either. I sit down on the stairs and lean my head against the wall. Half of me wants to be there, knowing what's said, and half doesn't.

They go into the kitchen. There's the sound of the kettle being filled. It's like listening to a play on the radio. Their voices come through the open door. Mum starts going over yet again what happened on Wednesday night. Dad had a booking for ten thirty. Take a man from outside The Squire Bassett pub to a house in Thorney, quite a good length journey. All straightforward. No reason to be worried. Bill always takes—took—sensible precautions, knew what he was doing. By now I could have written the script. Mum has this compulsion to go over everything again and again and again. Henry is very patient and makes the right noises in the right places. I suddenly realize he must be devastated too but whenever he comes he's supporting us. I suppose he goes home and Ginny supports him.

Mum suddenly starts on something new and I start

listening properly, slide down the stairs a bit to hear better. The police have been round while I was out. I suppose she didn't tell me because Short John was here and she'd probably just told him, or perhaps she didn't want to tell him, or perhaps she didn't want to tell me.

Dad died because he didn't have his seat-belt clipped in.

Dad was fanatical about seat-belts. He always wore his. He always made his passengers wear theirs. He wouldn't move the car an inch unless everyone was belted up.

It didn't make sense.

I miss the next bit of what Mum's saying but I catch the next bombshell.

His car was deliberately set light to. It wasn't an accident: the car setting itself on fire. Someone poured petrol on the seats and then chucked a match in. With Dad inside.

'He was already dead, thank God,' Mum says. Thank God? Where was God when all this was happening? I'd be prepared to thank God if Dad was sitting in the kitchen now. Perhaps I should have thanked God all the times he was there instead of taking it for granted. Perhaps God thought I was too ungrateful after He'd given me one of the best dads he'd got available.

And the police have arrested someone. Tony Lomond who owns Tony's Taxis on the other side of the town. 'They've got two witnesses who saw him behaving strangely in Grafton just about the same time Bill was driving through. And one of them saw him driving very fast towards Thorney. Road rage, they think. It would explain why the car was burnt. He must have hoped to destroy the evidence.'

Road rage! Another of Dad's obsessions. He always said it took two to rage and never answered back or blew his horn or made rude signs. He always apologized, especially when it wasn't his fault. 'I'm a professional,' he'd say. 'It's a jungle out there,' he'd say, 'and you don't provoke the wild animals. Just keep calm and feel superior to the poor things. Be professional.'

He died from road rage when he wasn't wearing his seat-belt. It doesn't make sense. It doesn't make sense at all.

'I haven't told Charley,' Mum says. Yes you have, I think, but in the best way, so that I don't have to react in front of you, don't need to think about you before I show my feelings. 'I didn't tell John either. I couldn't somehow.'

'Is he going on about selling again?' Henry asks. 'He's a bit pushy.'

'I think he means to be kind,' Mum says. Gullible Mum, never thinks ill of anyone. 'But it's too soon. Everyone says I mustn't make any decisions about anything for at least six months.'

'At least,' Henry agrees.

'But if the business runs down it won't be worth anything in six months and I don't know if I've got the heart to keep it going. If I try and make a mess of it, we won't have anything left and all Bill's hard work will have gone for nothing. I couldn't bear that. The funny thing is, Charley's desperate I do keep going. She wouldn't take any interest when Bill was alive. He wanted to teach her to drive on the old airfield track but she said she didn't want to. Now she's really upset if I talk of selling.'

'I expect she feels a bit guilty, a bit sorry she didn't share more with her dad. That's a normal feeling. But she's right at the moment. We can keep the business going between us for a while at least. Amit will be a tower of strength. Give you time to work out what'll be best.'

Mum starts crying again. I creep up to my room and lie on my bed and stare at the ceiling. How am I going to pass the time? Mum thinks I should go to school; that it will help if I can just get there. She's probably right. It certainly ought to help by giving me things I have to do but I can't go. I can't tell her the real reason, either. Kylie and her little gang.

I had been thinking I'd go to school. I nearly got there. I rang Amy and asked her to call for me so there was someone I could walk in with. She'd been round to see me at the weekend so we'd got over the embarrassment bit and she'd offered to come for me if I wanted, just ring any morning before eight fifteen. So I did this morning. We got as far as the corner of Hayling Road when Kylie and her mates caught us up.

'Did you hear about the Scottish taxi driver?' Kylie said, nice and loud and clear. 'Cremated himself to save paying an undertaker.' Her mates laughed like they always do when Kylie starts on someone. I turned round suddenly and caught her off balance so that she fell to the pavement and then I walked briskly towards home. Amy ran after me, 'Charley! Wait!'

'I'm not coming,' I said.

'Don't let her beat you. She's not worth it.' Amy was great. You might have thought she'd be glad that Kylie's usual Paki jokes had been given a rest.

I shook my head. 'Another day. I'll ring you.'

'I'll tell Miss Kirk,' she said. 'She's gone too far.' She always goes too far, I thought and realized that Amy had been like Dad: a professional in the jungle of the school playground.

'Go on,' I said. 'You'll be late.' She went to school and I went to put flowers on the place where Dad was killed and now I know more than I want about how he died and none of it makes any sense at all.

I lie on my bed staring at the ceiling and it all goes round and round in my head. I feel the ghouls circling, circling, and the vultures, and the bullies. That boy, and Short John, and Kylie: all of them circling, looking for weaknesses. Waiting to pounce, to suck tears into their cruel mouths.

I'll beat them, somehow.

I don't believe that Dad would drive without his seat-belt on. I don't believe he'd provoke a road-rage attack.

Why *was* that boy there? He didn't look like a ghoul. He looked embarrassed, sad. What did he mean about the tracks? I'll go and look tomorrow.

6
Simon

On Wednesday I got frightened, really frightened. I had been worried on Tuesday after Dad was arrested, worried sick, but I learnt on Wednesday that that was a different feeling altogether, and I learnt that one feeling doesn't cancel another out. It may lie on top of it, hide it for the moment, but it doesn't make it disappear.

I noticed the car when I looked out of the window at the rain falling again. It's what I do first every morning. I open the curtains, shut the window, and stare out. I'm not sure why and it seems to irritate Mum if she catches me at it. I think it's seeing the routine of life going on: the same people at the same time each day. Now that a bomb had suddenly gone off and blown my life apart so that I wasn't quite sure where the pieces were even, certainly couldn't start picking them up . . . now there was an awful fascination in seeing other people going about their lives as if nothing was different.

The BMW was different. It was parked on the other side of the road, about four houses down. It was slumming it a bit here, this is Escort territory, at best, and so it stood out. If people had rich relations come they didn't leave their cars out in the road. Mr Earnley opposite always moved his old Panda out into the road when his brother was coming with his Jag.

Because it was down the road I could see the man sitting behind the wheel, reading a newspaper. I stepped back, next to the curtain. This was the third time I'd seen that car, that man. He had threatened me, he had destroyed evidence, and now he was waiting outside my house. This couldn't be coincidence. I don't know why I knew it was me he was waiting for. The obvious thought would have been that this was Dad's house and it was nothing to do with me at all but the fear gripped me now and didn't let go until the whole thing was over.

I tried to tell myself this was silly. There was no way he could have known who I was when he saw me watching him yesterday, no way. There was no one to ask. The only people who had any idea where I was were the women in the shop and that girl, Mr Westcot's daughter. None of them knew me. Only the girl and the man knew I thought there was something funny about the tyre tracks. I didn't know what I knew either. It didn't make sense to me. Someone must think I knew more than I did. No one knew I'd seen the car, did they?

My thoughts were running round and round in my head, becoming more and more confused. I stood staring out of the window at the man in the BMW. The man in the BMW sat reading his newspaper. Normal, everyday life passed by, just as it did every day. Mum called me for breakfast, just as she did every day. Today she was brisk and efficient, acting herself but a bit unconvincingly. She said she'd drop me off at school on her way to the solicitor's as she didn't want me cycling in this rain—the sort of thing a concerned mother is supposed to say. She fussed in the past, she used to irritate me by fussing, but her heart was in it then. I told her I'd arranged to meet Dan outside the library, so she said she'd drop me there, all without the usual interrogation. As we drove down the road I looked in the wing mirror and saw the BMW do an efficient three-point turn and follow us. I wished mine were that neat.

Dad had started taking me to the unofficial driving school on the old airfield on Sunday mornings. He said that the younger you started driving the easier it came. They were great mornings, what people call quality time. I had his full attention and quite early on his full approval. He said I was a natural. It was a great feeling, in control of that power in the empty stretches of the runways. That was the only time you could be sure there wouldn't be kids in stolen cars bombing around. They always slept in on Sundays, occasionally, very occasionally, in police cells. In police cells . . . Everything kept coming back to the same ache.

Luckily it was an early opening morning at the library. If it had been one of the days it didn't open at all I'd have been stuck. I carefully turned and waved goodbye to Mum and saw out of the corner of my eye the BMW pull in to the kerb. The librarian greeted me like an old friend and I took a local history book and the Ordnance Survey map off the shelf and sat facing the window. I felt safe for the moment, but I couldn't stay here all day. I was better equipped than I had been on Tuesday. My school bag sat at my feet and held:

—one packed lunch (official Mother Issue)
—extra supplies (sneaked in while she was upstairs)
—camera
—notebook and pencil
—library ticket.

What I didn't have was my bike. I'd have to go home and fetch that, and that was the problem. I could see the BMW at the kerb still, the driver behind a newspaper. I could see myself walking out of the library, walking towards home then cycling, followed all the way at a discreet distance until the moment was right, out on that quiet country road.

The mangled body of Simon Lomond was discovered yesterday morning on the Thorney road. He was the victim of a hit-and-run accident and the police are baffled. He was found near the spot where the burnt-out car and body of Bill Westcot were discovered last week. Simon's father has been accused of that murder but police are ruling out any connection between the two crimes. 'It was a tragic accident and the driver must have panicked when he saw what he had done.' The police are appealing for witnesses. The police are not releasing details but the boy is believed to have met an extremely unpleasant death, parts of his body having been forced through his bicycle . . .

I was not getting on my bike with that man watching me.

It was beginning to look as though I was trapped, that it would be a question of whose nerve broke first, or whose bladder. I had to be ready in case he out-waited me and I had to go. What I needed then was to get him following me in his car, and then to be able to go somewhere he couldn't follow and disappear while he was parking his car.

The local history book had a recommended walk round the town, which started from the library. I studied it carefully and worked out a perfect route that would take me in a great loop home. I'd start as if going to school so that he wouldn't guess where I was really aiming for and then come out of the side door of Fenniman's and cut back through the multi-storey car park. I might as well go now. I had this vision of him coming into the library and pretending to be a teacher from school and dragging me off as a truant.

I took the map over to the desk with my library card and had it stamped out. It was then I had the brilliant idea. I would pick up today's newspaper from home when I got my bike. When I got home. The librarian smiled. I took a deep breath and walked out into the street, carefully not looking at the BMW, although out of the corner of my eye I saw a flash of white as if a newspaper had been put down. I turned towards school and walked as jauntily along as I could manage, which wasn't very jaunty. I must have looked a very reluctant student. There was enough traffic to drown out any one noise and I didn't dare turn round. I must be safer if he doesn't know I know he's following me; it must give me the edge.

It was so hard just walking along, not knowing what was happening behind me. I was really scared, getting more scared each step of the way, and wanting desperately to turn and see, but knowing I mustn't. I tried to use shop windows as mirrors like they do in films but it didn't work because they were all facing the wrong way. It seemed for ever along the pavement. I walked as far from the kerb as I could but there were other people who all seemed to have the same idea: old people dawdling, mothers with pushchairs rushing late to school, workers with brief-cases setting out on their day's business. The rain was still falling, though more gently now, and it made everyone keep their heads down or hide behind umbrellas so no one was looking where they were going. It became a nightmare in which I felt myself being pushed steadily, steadily towards the edge, and over it and under the wheels . . .

I darted into Fenniman's doorway and pushed.

Nothing moved. 'It's no good pushing that door, love.'
An old dear standing behind me. She reached out her
hand and tapped on the glass in front of my face:

STAFF TRAINING
The store will open at 9.30
on Wednesdays.
Fenniman's regret any inconvenience
to our customers.

'I don't know why they bother,' she was saying, 'I've
never seen any sign that they're trained in anything
except leaning on the counters and giggling with each
other.'

I looked at my watch. They should be open any
minute. What to do? Go round the side into the car
park? If I did that he'd know what I was doing for sure.
Wait here? Wait for him to pull in at the kerb, stride
across the pavement and drag me into his car before
anyone realized what was happening? And if they did,
they'd be too scared to do anything anyway. The old
dear might bash him with her handbag; she looked fierce
enough.

I turned my back on the door and faced the road.
There was the BMW just pulling in. I nearly ran for it
but summoned up every bit of courage I had. I smiled at
her. 'At least we're sheltered in here,' I said.

'Shouldn't you be in school?' she sniffed.

'Teachers' training day.'

She actually smiled at that. 'Typical,' she said.
'Everyone's training and leaving us to stand around
getting wet. Perhaps you'll have brilliant teachers
tomorrow.' I managed to laugh, trying to look as though
I was chatting happily with my granny. 'In my day,' she
started and I looked really interested.

Out of the corner of my eye I saw the door of the
BMW opening and started to panic seriously. I put my
hand on the woman's arm as if to hide behind her as I'd
always been protected by Granny. She looked down as
though I was one of those child muggers her newspaper
was probably always going on about and drew herself
together. I knew her handbag would be crashing into the
side of my head at any moment. If I ran it would be
straight into the BMW man, and she wouldn't stop him
now. If I stayed I'd be concussed and then dragged off
into the waiting car. I was cornered, done for. I stepped
back away from the pair of them.

'Sorry to keep you waiting,' came a bright voice as the
doors opened at last. 'Welcome to Fenniman's.'

7
Charley

I can't believe it! That boy. Here. Again.

I push my bike into the gateway just before the corner and crouch down. It's stopped raining, thank goodness, but the grass is sopping and the bottom of my jeans darken. It won't be long before damp soaks through my trainers and I get wet feet, which I hate. But I must know what he's doing.

I begin to wonder if he's a nutter. You think of them as old men with wild beards who wander the street shouting, but perhaps you get them young these days. Part of 'The Breakdown of Society' Mum's comforters are always going on about, with 'That Thatcher Woman' often mentioned in the same breath. He's not shouting and he hasn't got a beard—too young anyway—and he doesn't look like a nutter, quite the opposite if I'm honest. But he is behaving in a very odd way.

He's obsessed with those marks on the verge he was looking at yesterday. He's got a backpack today. He takes out of it, I don't believe it!, a newspaper. He puts it on the ground by the marks. He takes a camera out. He takes photographs. I suddenly realize what the newspaper's for. I've seen hostages holding newspapers on the news. It's to establish the date.

He must think he's a boy detective.

He puts the paper and camera in his backpack, gets on his bike and cycles on towards . . . towards . . . towards where it happened. I don't want him to see me. I want to see what he's doing. I wait until he's out of sight and ride slowly after him, stopping before each bend and peering round. I find another gateway that's just safe and push my bike behind the hedge. Then I realize I can walk along the field side of the hedge. There's a narrow strip of long wet grass between the hedge and the crop, whatever it is, in the field. It means wet feet and soaking jeans, but it also means I should be invisible.

It's not as easy walking silently through wet grass as you might think so I have to go slowly. I worry about the hedge as well. First I worry that he'll see me through it and then I worry that I won't be able to see anything when I get there. And all the time I wonder what I'm doing anyway. Isn't the whole thing sick?

Eventually I find I'm about opposite where it happened. I crouch down so that the wet grass is now fingering my bottom and find a thinnish part of the hedge. I can see, just, past the brown hawthorn stems, over the verge. The boy has his back to me and is sort of hunched over. I realize suddenly what he's doing. He's photographing the ground again. I bet he's got his newspaper there. He bends down. He has this obsession with tyre tracks and it's all a mystery to me.

There's the sound of a car and he looks up and round and I see his face and he looks terrified. Then the tension goes out of him and he picks up his backpack and puts it on. He's still got his camera in his hand and he sort of grins feebly as the car sweeps past. I'm getting cramp in my thighs so I straighten up cautiously and move a bit.

There's the sound of another car. I hear a sort of cry through the hedge and duck down quickly and look. The boy has gone. I curse and stand up and push my hands through the hedge to get a better view. Thorns draw a line of bright blood along my hands. The boy is running for a gap in the hedge opposite. His bike is lying on the verge. This big car screeches up, straight on to the bike. Stops on top of it. The driver bursts out shouting: 'Come here, you!' The boy's through the hedge gap and running like mad across the field.

Short John stands in the gap, shouting after him. There's no way he could catch the boy and he obviously knows it. The boy reaches the far corner of the field and clambers over a gate and drops out of sight. He's safe and I start to worry about me now. I stand absolutely still.

Short John walks back towards his car. He bends down and I see he's got my bunch of flowers from yesterday in his hand. He suddenly chucks them over the hedge. They separate in the air and scatter as they fall. One freesia ends up on the very top of the hedge like an exotic bloom. He gets back into his car and sits there for a moment. Then he starts his engine and drives his car backwards and then forwards and then backwards and then forwards over the boy's bike. Then his tyres squeal on the tarmac and he's gone and I can hear birds singing.

I find I've been holding my breath and now let it out. I'm shaking and I'm very, very angry. Whatever the boy was doing, there was no need to wreck his bike like that, in a fit of rage. And Dad's flowers, scattered, flung away as rubbish. I lick the blood off my hands and find I'm crying and wish I wasn't.

I walk back through the wet grass and on to the road. The boy's bike is a mess. I pick it up and carry it to the gap he disappeared through and prop it against the hedge as best I can. The wheels are bent and one pedal's snapped off and the gears are just hopeless. He won't be riding it again. I feel sorry for him for a moment and then I remember he's a ghoul at best and think he's perhaps deserved it.

There's no sign of him. It looks as though he's climbed over into the bridleway I can see going off. I might as well follow him and find out what's going on. Something is, for sure.

The rain clouds have cleared away and it's a bright morning now and the hawthorn's in full bloom. There

41

must be a good walk round here. Dad would have liked it. After sitting in a taxi all day he had to get out and walk, as far from cars and roads as possible, carrying his camera with all the fancy gear he loved. The ground's a bit muddy which slows me down and I get off and push the last bit of the hill. At the top there's a crossroads but I can see the boy walking downhill to the left. There are some farm buildings at the bottom but there is just a footpath down and I decide to leave my bike at the top and walk down. I'm not really convinced I want to catch him up but I do want to know what he's doing so I follow him.

When I get to the stile I'm glad I haven't ridden down. Walking was difficult enough and I'm soaked through from the knees down and quite miserable. I haven't seen the boy since I left the top but that probably means he hasn't seen me either and doesn't know I'm following him.

Until I fall over him.

Someone like God would have a good laugh here; someone looking down. There I was, first, crouching behind a hedge watching the boy. Then, there's the boy crouching down behind a hedge watching something and me walking up and sprawling over him, flat on my face in the wet grass. Soaked all over.

'Sssh!' the boy goes, pulling a face at me and pointing towards the buildings. I raise myself up on my elbows and look where he's pointing. There's Short John's car parked in the farmyard. It looks out of place: bright and rich and shiny in the middle of those derelict buildings and the rusty machinery.

'Where is he?' I whisper.

'Behind the barn,' he whispers back.

We both stay crouched down, staring, silent.

Nothing happens for a bit. I begin to feel stupid. Who is this boy? What is going on? Short John's a friend of the family. Then I see again him throwing the flowers, smashing the bike. I'm confused, lost.

Short John comes round from the back of the barn. He looks around, carefully, as if searching for something, or someone. He takes a half-step towards where we're hiding and then turns and gets into his car and drives off. There's a sharp turn round the barn and his car's out of sight and the engine noise fades. I stand up and look down at the boy.

'Who are you?' I ask.

8
Simon

'Who are you?' she asked.

I hadn't realized until then that she didn't know who I was and felt suddenly awkward. 'My father killed your father' didn't seem quite the best introduction.

'I'm Simon,' I said.

She looked at me helplessly.

'I'm sorry about your father,' I said, and stopped. I couldn't go on to the next bit, couldn't say who I was. 'I want to show you something,' I said. 'In the barn.' I walked through the gateway and stood in the farmyard waiting for her to come with me. She just stood there.

'Why are you doing this?' she asked. 'Why is Short John so angry? He wrecked your bike after you ran off, you know.'

'There's something funny going on,' I said. 'I need to find out what. It's not right, what they're saying.'

She stared at me. 'Was it your father?' she asked.

I nodded. 'But he didn't do it.'

That seemed to set her off and she raged at me. She was higher up the hill and seemed to tower over me and she glowed with anger. 'Your father is an animal, worse than an animal. He just killed Dad for no reason at all.'

'He wouldn't.'

'Listen to me!' she shouted. 'Just listen to a few facts. Your father drove to Grafton that night, didn't he? Didn't he?'

'Yes, but . . . '

'Don't "but" me. He drove to Grafton and he was behaving like a maniac. He was seen! He was seen by two separate witnesses. Two! Driving like a madman.

44

How many maniacs do you think you get on that road at night? Hundreds? It was your father, out of control.'

I stared at her and the worm of doubt wriggled again inside me, the nagging thoughts I had needed to suppress. Up to now I had convinced myself that Dad couldn't have done such a thing but her words broke through that conviction. Mum always said Dad should never have been a taxi-driver. He didn't have the temperament. He hadn't wanted to be, music was his passion, but he always said he hadn't had the breaks, that he had responsibilities. The traffic got to him, the jams, the noise, the fumes. He disliked his fares: rude or drunk, he said. He was his own boss but at everyone's command; all the worry but none of the independence.

And he had a temper. When he was tired, he'd snap, flare up, hit out. And then be very sorry afterwards.

Could this be simple road rage? He'd had a long day; it was a late trip. Too profitable to turn down, but perhaps one drive too many. Suppose he'd lost his temper for a moment. Just one moment, and lashed out. An unlucky blow can kill. People can have thin skulls, heart attacks. Then what do you do? It's too late to say 'Sorry' and be forgiven. It's done now. Giving himself up would help no one, would just ruin three lives, pointlessly. Set light to the car and drive away as if nothing had happened. And try to live with it.

The girl was standing on the bank above me, crying. 'He couldn't have done it,' I said, but without conviction now.

'Shut up! Shut up!' she shouted and turned and stumbled back up the path. I looked after her. I couldn't go after her, she hated me, and with reason. She'd said my bike was smashed. If I went through the buildings and turned left on the road I'd get to my bike after she'd left. See what the damage was. I was shaking suddenly, afraid of my thoughts.

I turned and walked slowly past the buildings. I

remembered I had meant to show her the car hidden in the barn. I didn't understand what was going on. If Dad had killed her father, what was the man she'd called Shotgun doing with the tyre tracks, doing in these buildings, and threatening me? Did she know him?

I went into the barn. The car was still there. I took photos until the flash stopped working: general views, number plates, the dent. I wasn't sure what I was seeing, what it meant, but—like the rubbed-out tyre marks—it must mean something important or it wouldn't be hidden here. I was tempted to search it but worried about leaving my fingerprints on it, or destroying evidence. I did peer through all the windows but couldn't see anything I thought was significant. I did see the key in the ignition and thought for a wild moment of driving the car away, delivering it to the police station and demanding the release of my dad, but I knew that was just silly.

I walked out into what was now bright sunlight and was temporarily dazzled. I looked up the path in case that route was clear but I can't have been as long as I had thought taking the photographs. The girl was near the top of the hill, her back to me, walking slowly up. I guessed she'd stop at the top to draw breath, turn round, and look back. I didn't want her to see me staring back at her. I'd go the other way then.

I rounded the corner of the barn, and was grabbed. A carrier-bag over my head and arms round my body. For a moment I froze and then sucked in a great mouthful of air to scream. The plastic of the bag went into my mouth, was sucked against my nose. I couldn't breathe. I couldn't move my hands to tear the bag away. The more I tried to breathe the tighter the plastic moulded itself to my face. I felt faint, went limp.

The bag was pulled away from my mouth and held while I drank in air in great gasps that shook my body. 'Try shouting and that's how you'll die,' said the voice that had shouted at me twice before, the voice of the man the girl called Shotgun. 'Now walk!'

He half pushed and half carried me across the farmyard. Light came through the white plastic and I thought I could make out shapes, and then a darkness. I was pushed suddenly, violently, and lost my balance and fell sprawling, cascading into metal that clanged and banged. Pain jolted through my knee. I heard the scraping of wood and the darkness became more complete. I ripped the carrier-bag off my head. 'Good Food Costs Less.' Not a very helpful message.

I was in a wooden shed. Sunlight came in dusty rods through chinks in the walls. Around me was farm rubbish: empty drums, rusty machinery, plastic sacks. I felt for injuries but there was no blood and nothing shrieked at me. Even my knee didn't feel too bad now. I got up and moved towards the door and found a hole big enough to look through. It gave me a view down the farm track. It gave me a view of a BMW driving away. Then it gave me a view of empty countryside.

I tried other holes in other walls. I had a comprehensive view of the buildings and of the fields, and of the total lack of people. I wasn't sure whether this was comforting or not. One thing was certain: at the moment I was on my own. Another thing was certain: I had no idea at all how long I would be left. For ever? Until plans could be made to dispose of me? I rattled the door but it seemed to have been tied shut, to keep me secure.

I knew what I had to do. Anyone who's read any books or watched any TV would know what to do:

> Situation: locked in.
> Solution: break out.

And this time it should be easy. Old wooden shed. Old tools, metal tools. Recent school lessons on levers including a riot on the see-saw at the Rec. With one bound our hero would be free.

It wasn't quite that easy, of course, and I learnt how careless about detail writers are, how many stories are conjuring tricks. You're not meant to notice what's impossible. It would be more honest to issue:

Instructions for Escaping from a Shed

1. Start by selecting a suitable shed. Time spent on preparation at the beginning is time saved in the long run. Many beginners have chosen quite unsuitable sheds and have learnt the hard way. It is essential to have an old shed in poor repair. It is also necessary to find one that has a wide selection of farm tools. Inspect any shed you are offered carefully before accepting it. Unscrupulous dealers may try to off-load unsuitable sheds on unwary novices.
2. Find your lever. This needs to be something with a thin enough end to wedge between the boards that make up the shed walls, long enough to multiply the force you are able to apply, yet rigid enough not to bend under your weight and leave you nose down on the floor. Again, time spent searching the shed at this stage will save accidents and frustration later. It is important not to give up hope. If you have chosen the right shed, there will be the right lever. It's just a matter of recognizing it.
3. Give up the whole scientific plan and just bash frantically at the back wall until the planks splinter and you can push desperately out, scratching yourself as you go.

At the time I panicked badly. It's one of the many things about that time that I try not to remember, that lurk in my nightmares. I hear myself screaming, howling. I see myself smashing blindly, wildly, at the wall until at last I break through, burst out of the darkness into the blinding light. I see myself standing in the sunshine, panting, shaking. Then I wake up, panting, shaking.

For some reason I desperately mended the hole I had smashed in the rotting wooden planks of the shed, thinking that an irate farmer with a shotgun would suddenly appear. The thing about breaking old weathered wood is, you can push the jagged ends together so that you'd hardly know they'd been broken. I took pride in what I'd done, stood back and admired it, and remembered I'd left my backpack inside.

I had just enough self-control not to howl, not to rip the shed wall apart again. I walked round to the front and saw the door had been fastened with a twisted piece of wire. It took seconds to untwist it. It took longer to force myself to go back into the shed, to grab my backpack and dart out again. I left the door open, as if I had been rescued by an accomplice. If my captor ever returned, it would give him something to think about.

I looked around. I seemed to be the only person left in the world. The farm track worried me so I set off on the footpath, back up the hill, back to my wrecked bike.

9
Charley

It's a steeper climb up the hill than I had realized and it's warm in the sun. I stop for a breath and turn and look back. The farmyard is empty, decaying quietly all by itself. I go on and don't let myself stop again until I reach the top.

This time there's a figure: the boy. Nosing about like a prime ghoul, though goodness knows what he expects to find down there. He walks away and then suddenly he's leapt on. Something white goes over his head and he's being forced into one of the buildings. The door's slammed. The figure bends down and then straightens up and does something with the door.

It's Short John, I realize. I'm torn now. I hate that boy. I would love to push him into a shed and lock the door and leave him screaming in the darkness, hammering his hands against the walls until the blood flows, sinking down in utter hopelessness. Let him try the cold and windy blackness I have been thrown into. Let his murdering father hear in his cell that a terrible vengeance has fallen on his son.

But I loathe Short Slimy John, and, worse, distrust him. Something is up and I don't know what. I stand indecisive on the hilltop and in the end timidity wins. I can't believe, quite, that Short John would do that boy serious harm but if he could, he'd do it to me too.

I grab my bike and bump precariously fast down the hill and on to the road. I pedal hard until I reach Grafton, flinching at each passing car in case it's Short John. I'm exhausted when I reach the village. I notice someone's been round delivering the free newspaper and has left them sticking half out of letter boxes to

50

encourage the burglars. The Neighbourhood Watch, who have a threatening sign at the entrance to the village, can't be too pleased. There's a twee row of thatched cottages whose doors open straight on to the pavement. I do my bit by taking one of the copies out of a letter box and dropping it into my basket.

MURDER LATEST

screams up at me. Am I never to escape?

I see the church and decide to go in to rest for a bit. I've been shaken by what's happened this morning. The door stands open, inviting, trusting. It's cool and quiet inside and my trainers are soundless on the tiles as I walk to the front pew. I kneel in what's becoming my usual place and try to let the peace soak into me.

We're occasional churchgoers: Christmas, Easter, Harvest—that sort of thing. Social. There's no religion at home, no talk of God. The vicar came round: to condole and to console, he said. He seemed pleased with the phrase, but may have been well-meaning. I hate being in my room, on my own, but here I feel more calm. Granny would have liked this church. It's like the one we went to when I stayed with her when I was little: the service full of candles and smoke and bright colours and singing. There's the echo of incense here and little lights burning.

I stayed with Granny the year before she died suddenly. It was years later that I learnt it was her money that had let Dad give up the job he hated and start his taxi business: just him first and then the gradual expansion to three cars. Enough, he said, to provide a 24-hour 365-day service and work for all at the busiest times of day, but not so big that the business became a monster that took over his life. That was what he always said: I've grown to a comfortable size.

He had loved his taxis: loved driving well, meeting people, the lack of routine, the regulars and the unexpected, being out in the middle of life going on, hustle and bustle. He always had a stream of stories about his day: all rather larger than real life, I thought. Some of them involved beautiful women in distress and him as the knight in the shining cab. Mum pretended to be jealous but he'd say, 'I haven't time, I haven't time— more's the pity!' and she'd pretend to bash him. If another woman had lured him away, at least I'd still see him. Any woman but Death.

I hadn't liked the business. It was the centre of his life, where I should have been. He'd rush off when we were doing something together, saying: 'Sorry, darling, duty's calling!' He always looked pleased to be going. I worried about road accidents. Some of his stories were about crashes, wrecks, he'd seen. When I was younger he'd tell Mum in the kitchen, not knowing I was on the stairs, listening, worrying about his safety. He was a fanatic for courtesy and carefulness but the roads are full of idiots. There was one on the TV last week: driving on the M4 at ninety miles an hour, on his mobile, and making notes on a pad. What's the use of courtesy and care with him around?

The business had been his life and with his death it must not die, be swallowed up. Mum sees Short John as caring, considerate, concerned. I know he is slimy, shifty, sham.

In the quiet of the church resolution hardens in me. We will keep the business going. I will find out what is going on.

What *is* going on? That boy, Simon, had said something about wanting to show me something in the barn. Short John had been there. Why? Why was he so angry with the boy? I hadn't stopped to think before. Now, none of it makes much sense at all. And the boy is locked in the shed. What am I going to do about that?

I look up at the cross on the altar and know I can't leave him there. I can ring the police but I don't think I can face that. And there'll be so many questions. And Mum will have to be involved. And Short John . . .

I'll go back, carefully. See what's going on. See what's in this barn.

I leave the church reluctantly, go out into the sun and the observing world and cycle wearily back, look forward to that long free-wheel down from the village.

In the distance I see a figure, bent over a bike, pushing it up the hill towards me. I don't want to speak to him. My conscience is now clear. I turn sharply and pedal back until I'm back at the church. I hide my bike behind the graveyard wall and sit behind a tombstone. It takes a long time for him to come. He's half-carrying, half-dragging his bike. He looks dishevelled, fed-up.

I watch him pass and suddenly feel bone tired, too tired to care about anything except getting home. I'll give him time to get clear first. I lean back against the stone and doze off in the sun, feeling like a corpse that's resurrected too early on Judgement Day.

MURDER LATEST

Police are now holding a suspect in the 'Road Rage' murder case that has shocked the community—and it's looking worse and worse. Major crime has hit our peaceful community.

Inspector Mopper would say only that a man was 'helping with enquiries'—the phrase police always use when they believe they have caught the villain.

A police source admitted they were holding Tony Lomond, owner of Tony's Taxis, but refused to link him directly with the crime.

The victim, popular Bill Westcot, was a rival taxi proprietor and ran Westcot Cabs. His body was found in his burnt-out taxi on the Grafton to Thorney road late last Wednesday night.

Police have not released their post-mortem findings but do not believe it was an accident.

Tony Lomond, 40-year-old father of one, lives with his wife Janet at 65 Forest Rd. His business has expanded steadily since he started it eight years ago.

Bill Westcot was well-known in the community for his charity work with disabled children. Mrs Grace Stibb, speaking for the Activities for Children Trust (ACT) which arranges a wide variety of adventurous activities for children said he would be badly missed. 'What sort of evil man could do something like this to Bill?'

10
Simon

I thought things were bad before.

I had no idea.

I had no idea people could hate so much. Or that it would hurt so much.

It started with the phone calls. We had two phones: our private line, which wasn't listed so that our private calls wouldn't get mixed up with work ones, and the business line. Mum answered the first call. She wouldn't tell me what was said, just stood there white-faced and shaking, and then she went out of the house and down the garden and leant on the shed.

The first one I answered was from a nicely-spoken woman. She told me exactly what she thought of my father, in clear, chilly words and then put the phone down.

The next, a man, shouted and swore.

As soon as I put the phone down, it rang again. And again. Hatred flowed out and swamped me and the phone had me trapped. I had to pick it up each time it rang. And it rang and rang. The world was full of people who wanted to tell me what they thought of my dad. After for ever Mum came back and put her hand over mine as I was about to pick up the phone and switched on the answering machine to record a new message. 'Thank you for calling Tony's Taxis. I'm afraid we are not able to take calls or bookings at the moment.'

'Say something back on the tape,' I said. 'Why should they get away with it?'

She put her hand on my shoulder. 'There's no point in answering back. No one listens. There are a lot of sick people out there, but there might be genuine calls, or friendly ones. Let's be dignified, show we're superior, and time will show we're right.'

What time showed first was more, and more, hatred towards us. Letters shoved through the letter-box after dark. Letters through the post. Typewritten. Scrawled. Shouting out in red capital letters. Muck thrown into the front garden. Dog muck, and worse, from miles around ended up on our front path, slid down our windows, came through the letter box. After the first, Mum spread polythene to catch it but the house still stank.

Spray-can graffiti on the garden wall, on the front of the house.

'Sticks and stones,' Mum kept muttering, until the stones started and our windows shattered that Thursday night. It had been not much over twenty-four hours since the newspaper report but I had lived through lifetimes of hatred.

We came down to have a cup of tea, to sit together at the back of the house. With the side-gate bolted we felt more secure there. Mum had rung the police and they'd said they'd send a car round as soon as they could but they were busy that evening.

It went quiet at last and we cleared up the glass from the front rooms: shards of glass smeared with muck. 'We'll go to Gran's,' Mum said.

'Suppose they follow us there? What if they do this to her house?' We looked at the ruin of home and thought of Gran's neat, cared-for house.

'You go to Gran,' Mum said.

'I'm not leaving you,' I said. 'You always told me to face up to bullies. And it's probably all over now. They've had their fun. They'll leave us alone.'

They didn't.

11
Charley

I feel life's going round in one of those nightmare circles when Short John arrives, fresh from his bike-smashing and kid-shedding. He does the usual emotional greeting stuff and sits down at the kitchen table with Mum for the usual cup of coffee. I do the usual surly exit and sit out-of-sight on the stairs for the usual eavesdrop.

He does the usual commiseration bit, which means letting Mum go on and on and grunting in the right places. All credit to him here; I haven't the patience to cope with this. Then he moves inevitably into the selling the business routine, but this time there's a difference. It's stopped being just a favour to her. It seems it's a favour to him. I move down a stair and listen more carefully. If it's true, it's surprising. If it's true.

'I didn't want to say this before,' he says now, 'because I didn't think it would be fair. Things aren't going well at the moment at all.'

Mum makes some remark about what a wonderful business he has, how Dad always admired it, but her heart's not in it, I can tell.

'Was a wonderful business,' he says. 'Now I'm lucky if I can pay the wages. It's everything: taxis, hiring, funerals,' he adds with a singular lack of tact.

'Bill said business was good at the moment,' Mum says. Even better now in one department, I think.

'I'm getting paranoid,' he says. 'Taxi's booked, turns up and finds customer gone. Sometimes there's no one there at all; sometimes it seems another taxi's already been. Cars hired, then no one turns up.' He seems to remember at last he's doing Dad's funeral because he shuts up about them but I can't help wondering. Are the

57

corpses just not turning up as booked? Is a rival firm kidnapping them? Have people just stopped dying?

When I listen again he's talking about his suspicions, and he's linking his suspicions to Dad's death. 'It's part of a pattern,' he's saying, 'part of a pattern. He's expanding his business by any means: intercepting our radio calls, ambulance chasing, intimidation now. My guess is he just planned to frighten Bill but something went wrong. That boy of his has been behaving very suspiciously, too. I think he's been trying to destroy evidence.'

Mum says something about the police.

'It's just suspicions,' he says. 'I've got no proof, no proof at all. All I've done so far is give the boy a bit of a fright. I just got mad, fighting fog all the time.'

Mum clucks away a bit and changes the subject and he lets her. I go up to my room and lie on my bed and think. If anyone's behaving oddly, it's Short John. I'm not sure I buy his story at all. I suspect that, like a good liar, he's taking the truth and shifting it along a bit. Surely it would be a bigger firm doing the threatening? You don't often get the playground midgets doing the bullying. He's the one trying to take over the smaller outfit, one way or another . . .

And then the most enormous firework explodes in the sky and the whole landscape is lit up. He's responsible for Dad's death. He's framing Tony Lomond. He's trying to stop his son finding evidence of what he's done.

He'll end up with both businesses. One bought from a grieving widow, the other from the wife of a man serving a long prison sentence. The scheming, slimy beast.

And only the boy stands in his way.

The boy. Simon, he said he was.

I shut my eyes and play scenes through in my head. Short John shouting at the boy, running over his bike in rage. The boy, Simon, at the hedge above the old farm, wet-eyed, saying he's sorry about Dad, wanting to show me something, me shouting. Short John pushing him into a shed and me turning away. Me hiding behind a gravestone, seeing him dejected, pushing his wrecked bike.

I hear voices in the hall, the door. I get off my bed and look out of the window, sideways so I can't be seen. Short John's going down the path, to his shiny BMW. It doesn't look like the car of a man about to go bankrupt.

I flop back on my bed and stare at the ceiling again. If I'm right, Short John's cooked the whole thing up. If I'm right, it must work something like this:

RECIPE FOR TAKING OVER TAXI FIRMS

This basic recipe should enable you to gobble up two firms

at the same time: one firm neatly cooked by the other.

Ingredients
• a reasonable-sized town with several taxi firms,

yours rather bigger than the others

• a complete lack of scruples

• an accomplice

Method
• your accomplice books a taxi from Firm A

• you . . . you . . .

The only way I can think about this at all is to make it into a game of some kind, and even then I can't get past a certain point. But it all begins to make some sense now. I had been puzzled before about two things that were so unlike Dad that I thought they couldn't be true: him not wearing a seat-belt, and him getting involved in a road-rage incident. Now I can see how it all might have worked.

And how the plot develops. He now buys up Dad's firm out of kindness, to help Mum. Mr Lomond's firm either goes bust when he goes to prison, which removes the competition, or he can take it over at a rock-bottom price. He's swallowed two firms and is big enough to swamp the rest. No wonder he's so full of stories about dirty tricks, about taxi wars. But he's not the victim, oh no. He's the big bad wolf.

And only the boy stands in his way. The wet-eyed boy with the smashed bike.

And me, if I choose. If I dare. If I knew what to do. If I could face the police, with no evidence, just suspicions.

A hysterical teenage girl who's just lost her father. Give her a sedative.

Me and the boy together.

What did he want to show me?

I know where he lives; it was in the paper. I'll go round, apologize.

As soon as I turn the corner into his road I know, but I cycle slowly past all the same. Number sixty-five Forest Road has all its windows boarded up and its front garden is a mess. They've been driven out by the bullies.

Now it's just me.

But I can't.

TAXI DEATH: MAN CHARGED

Police investigating the death of Mr William Westcot on May 7th on the Thorney to Grafton road last night charged a man with his murder.

Anthony Lomond, of 65 Forest Road, will appear before magistrates today and the police will oppose bail.

Lomond, aged 40, is owner of a rival taxi firm and police are not ruling out a connection. At first it was believed to be a road-rage attack.

'We are keeping an open mind,' said Inspector Mopper, who is heading the inquiry. He appealed for any witnesses who were in the area on the Wednesday evening between 9 p.m. and midnight, or anyone who has any information.

Lomond's family have left their house after some trouble on Thursday when windows were broken. Inspector Mopper said the police could not condone lawless behaviour, but their resources were stretched.

16 Chidham Rd
Friday 16th

Dear Simon,

   I came to your house but it was all boarded
up and the paper today said you'd gone so I
don't know what to do. Your phone is switched
off too. I thought if I wrote this it might
get to you, I thought someone might be
collecting your letters.
   I am sorry I shouted at you on Wed. I thought
then that it was your father who had done it.
I don't think that now but I have no proof.
   Do you have any? What did you want to show
me? Please telephone me: 25571. *Please*.
   I don't know what to do.
   I am sorry.

                    Charley Westcot

12
Charley

The weather turns bright and warm, to mock me. My mood wants drenching rain and wind-swept moors lit momentarily by lightning and thunder echoing around. Instead it gets dusty suburban streets and the stink of traffic.

The police allow us to hold Dad's funeral.

I know that Short John killed him.

I don't hear from Simon.

Funerals: you see too many films with peaceful scenes in country churchyards under the rook-filled elms, coffins lowered into the welcoming earth and the grey-haired vicar reciting the beautiful old words while daffodils shine in the dewy grass. Mum wouldn't have a cremation, not after what's happened, she said, so we got the cemetery. Bleak bare rows of humps in the ground. Green plastic grass lining the hole. The vicar's banal words, today's empty flat supermarket words. And me? I wanted to be able to howl, to fling myself into the earth's ravening mouth, to rage against the dying of his light. I stood prim and correct by the plastic grass, dry-eyed, immobile.

Short John: a tower of strength, he's called, by everyone. A bare-faced scheming snake coiling and coiling, offering Mum the poisoned apple.

Simon: the tense, sad Simon I shouted at, his shocked face over his own hell. Lost somewhere out there in the world.

I flee the house when I can. I feel guilty doing it because I know Mum wants me there. I know too that instead of holding each other up we are dragging each other down, down into this dark pit that has no bottom, no place you can stop and rest and draw breath and then try to struggle up. We are drowning swimmers going under together into the silent under-water world. We mouth silently but nothing gets through.

Whenever Short John comes, I flee. Partly seizing my chance to break out into the outside world, partly running in terror from his bloody hands. I flee the town with its streets of metal coffins inching along, mouthing zombies upright within, fumes of death spewing out. I flee my own increasing despair.

I have two havens I flee towards. Grafton church comes first. I have learnt to love its cool peace, the hint of incense, the votive candle flames pale in the sunlight. I cannot bring myself to light a candle at the feet of the statue of the mother and child. My mother's hands are out to me, but as those of a drowning woman, and she can no longer rock my griefs away in her arms. But I take comfort from the little tongue of fire that dances so gently on the candle, as if it can do no harm at all.

The church pours peace into me, filling up the hole so that I can walk out on firm ground again. Sometimes that is as far as I go; sometimes it is enough. On other days, hotter and more sultry ones, I am restless still and ride on towards the hill top where there is always a faint breeze. Here the spread-out landscape makes it all unreal. I can look down to where Dad died, to the farm buildings that seem to hold a secret, and back towards home and an unspoilt life.

There is another reason, too, why I keep coming back to these two places. They were where I had met Simon, and they are where I hope to meet him again. He seems to hold the key to what has been going on. The farm buildings keep calling me, but I am scared to go on my own. I bring a book with me and read in the shade of the hedge until it is time to go home.

One afternoon, it must be about two weeks after I had last seen Simon, I can bear it no longer. I leave my bike at the top and push my way down the footpath. It has become totally overgrown and walking is slow and hot, which helps take my mind off my destination. I am fighting through the luxuriance of life to the hidden mystery: Ariadne facing the maze without Theseus. Burrs and goose-grass cling to my jeans, trying to hold me back. Hawthorn twigs scrape at my face, hoping to blind me.

I come to the gap where I had fallen over Simon, where we had seen Short John. The farmyard and its buildings are empty, peaceful, so peaceful I fear what might be hidden in the black hearts of the ruined barns.

It is difficult to step through that hedge-gap, to slither down the bank, to set the first foot on the cracked concrete of the yard. I have seen too many films in which nasty men grab the unsuspecting heroine. I don't believe that being a suspecting unheroine will stop me being jumped on suddenly. I want to cry out, 'Come on! Get me now; get it over with!' but daren't.

This is silly. I make myself walk into the nearest black mouth. It's just an empty barn. Sunlight arrows through holes in the wall, dust motes dance. As my eyes get used to the darkness I see the usual farm rubbish: rusty metal and torn plastic. If there's anyone here, he's well hidden. I glance quickly back over my shoulder in case someone's creeping up on me, but there's nothing. I make myself step into the barn, poke desultorily at the heaps. Nothing means anything. I don't know what I expect. Simon had found something. Short John was obviously excited enough to imprison him. That was a couple of weeks ago, I suddenly realize. Whatever might have been here will have gone by now.

That realization dispels all the figures lurking in the shadows. No one will waste their time here now. It is what it seems: a deserted farm. I turn my back on the gloom and step into the brightness, feeling silly. I walk briskly round the whole sad site: nothing, nothing, nothing. Imagined fears fed by grief and sleeplessness.

I look in the last barn and am turning to go back up

the hill to my bike when I realize and all the fearful
figures swoop back with shrieks of delight. I make
myself stop. Somehow I make myself take one step and
then another and then another, into the blackness.

There is a taxi, right at the back: interlaced TT on the
driver's door, big dent on the back door. TT: Simon's
father's taxi. The murder weapon.

I run as if all of hell is after me across the yard,
through the gap, up the hill. My foot catches and I fall
face down on the overgrown path. I lie panting,
expecting hands to grab me. My gasps for air and my
thumping heart deafen me so that I wouldn't even hear
them coming.

No one comes. My breath slows. I roll over, sit up.
Nothing has changed. A thought drops out of the clear
sky:

If it was Simon's father's taxi, why would he want to
show it to me?

I pick this thought up, turn it over in my hands, look
at it critically. I see no answer to it. I should go back
and look. But what would I be looking for? Simon must
have seen something that told him. If it isn't his father's,
whose is it? And if it is something to do with Dad's
death, then it is dangerous, terribly dangerous. To his
killer. To me. To Simon. This place is not an innocent
deserted farmyard. It is a booby-trap, waiting for me,
for him, to trip it.

I stand up and walk back up the hill. I look fearfully
over my shoulder every second step, look down at my
feet to make sure I don't trip again. As I get further
away panic grows in me as I realize how stupid I have
been. Simon escaped Short John somehow. The next
person caught would not find it so easy. I walk the last
few paces slowly, backwards. The ruins stay deserted.
Nothing moves. I realize I have been holding my breath
in and let it out with a great sigh.

A hand touches my shoulder.

13
Simon

I have never seen anyone jump like Charley did when I touched her. She started, turned, fell, all in one movement. She sat on the ground staring up at me. 'Where have you been?' she shouted. 'God, you frightened me!'

'I'm sorry. I only got your letter this morning. We've been away. I tried to ring but you weren't there. I came to look for you. I thought you might be here.'

She didn't seem to be going to stand up so I sat down beside her.

We had been to see Dad in prison yesterday. Mum hadn't taken me before. On remand, he was, but it seemed as if he was already convicted. He and Mum kept trying to pretend everything would be all right but I don't think they believed it. Then, yesterday, sitting in the visitors' room, with them falsely cheerful for me, I hadn't believed anything would be all right ever again. I despaired so totally I thought I must die. They were not them, they were shadows, unreal, empty. Now, today, sitting on the hill in the sunshine, I thought it all seemed impossible, unreal, a story.

'I saw the taxi,' she said. 'That's what you wanted to show me, isn't it?' I nodded. So it was still there. That surprised me. 'What does it mean?' she said. 'Isn't it your father's?'

'No, it isn't! I thought you believed he didn't do it. It's not his,' I said calmly, somehow. 'I know it's not his. The number plates are the same but it's not the same car.' I ticked facts off on my fingers. 'The seats are the wrong colour. There's no tachometer. There's no tin of sweets. The logo is badly painted. It's meant to look like his cab, but it isn't.'

'So someone set him up,' she said. 'I thought so. I know who did.'

'That man,' I said. 'The one who caught me. Shotgun.'

'Shotgun?' she asked, and then she laughed, really laughed. 'Short John,' she said. 'You know, sort of like Long John Silver. It's a private joke of mine.' I stared at her. The man hadn't looked at all like Long John Silver. 'Oh, it's silly,' she said. 'I'd been reading *Treasure Island* and he came in, John Hunston he is really, likes to be called Uncle John, and said, "Oh, isn't that a book for boys? I do hope you're not turning into a tomboy, Charlotte," all smarmy. And I thought: you're short, got two legs, no parrot, and you're not a pirate, but I still don't trust you an inch. So I started calling him Short John in my head. I like Shotgun, though.'

'So you think Shotgun did it?' I asked. I thought Short John made him sound cosy, and I didn't think he was cosy at all.

'He runs Caring Cars and he's trying to buy Dad's business off Mum, started even before the funeral. My dad dead, yours in prison—great boost for his business.'

'But killing?'

'Someone killed Dad,' she said. We sat in silence and I thought about what she said. It made sense.

'It's a lot of fuss for a few taxis,' I said.

'Remove the competition. It would more than double his income, treble it. That's quite a lot of money. And then he could expand into other towns.'

I still wasn't sure. I couldn't kill someone for money, but I knew from the papers that lots of people did.

'We have to tell someone now,' I said. 'Will you come and talk to my mum? I'm not walking into a police station. I've seen them on *The Bill*, sniggering away. We'll tell my mum and she'll deal with them, or tell her solicitor.'

'Yes,' she said. 'Let's do it.'

We bumped back down the bridle path and turned for

home along the road. I was riding Mum's old-fashioned thing and had trouble keeping up on the long hill into Grafton. At least I wasn't having to push my wrecked bike this time. Then I had a sense of time going round in a loop as a familiar black BMW swerved in and stopped in front of Charley.

Shotgun, Short John, leapt out of the driver's door and walked down the road towards her. She had stopped as soon as she saw him, but didn't turn away. The row had started before I caught up. She was screaming at him, really screaming. She'd totally lost it, was out of control.

He stepped towards her. She threw her bike at him, really threw it. She must have been wild with rage to have had the strength. It caught him off-balance and he fell on to the road with the bike on top of him. She went on screaming and moved towards him as if she was going to boot him or jump on top of the bike and push it through him.

I got off my bike and grabbed her, pulled her back somehow. I held her while she stood on the road and raged, her words making no sense. She suddenly stopped and just stood there crying, shuddering. He got up slowly, holding the bike away from him. He put it down gently on the verge and then stood, his hands out.

'What have I done?' he asked.

Charley was great then. I don't know how she did it at all. I couldn't have said anything. She shrugged my arms off her and raised her head and looked straight at him. 'You killed my father,' she said simply.

He stared at her then he turned and walked away, back towards his car. I saw her take in a deep breath and thought she was about to scream again so I put my hand out and touched her. She let it out slowly as he turned. He stood behind his car on the quiet country road and I was terrified.

He raised his hands into the air and dropped them slowly. 'I did what?'

'You killed my father, and you put the blame on his father. And we've got proof.'

'And why should I have done this?

'You want to buy Dad's firm.'

'Charlotte, I want to buy the firm to help your mother. It's cut-throat in the taxi business now. There's people trying to build empires by ruining us all, there's a war. Big firms are moving in. It's got so even I can hardly cope. Your dad was struggling. There's no way your mother could survive. Believe me.'

I almost did, he sounded so sincere. And it fitted with Dad's worries.

'My father didn't kill him,' I said.

'I couldn't believe he did,' he said. 'He's a decent bloke. But the police seemed confident. I just thought that he'd snapped suddenly under the pressure, or that it had been an awful accident. I know he's not behind any big plot, if there is one. Most days I think I'm paranoid.'

'You would say that, wouldn't you?' Charley said. 'But murderers aren't famous for their honesty.'

I saw him flinch at the word. I knew what it felt like to have 'Murderer!' spat at you, or shouted—'Murderer! Murderer! Murderer!'—like a nightmare playground chant.

He walked two paces back towards us. 'How can I convince you? I had nothing to do with it. You know me, Charley.'

That seemed to break something in her and she started screaming again, out of control. Most of what she said didn't make any sense, it was just abuse, filth thrown at him. I grabbed her again and he stepped back, raised his hands as if to push all that rage away from him. I realized that, however bad all this had been for me, it was far, far worse for her. Unimaginably worse.

I put my arm round her and pulled her away. She let me take her a few yards down the road. He just stood and watched, looking helpless. 'The car,' Charley said, and turned back towards him. 'What about that car then?' she yelled at him.

'Don't!' I said quickly, quietly. 'Don't say anything to him about the car or the barn. Not here. It's not safe.' I had a picture in my mind of him reversing his car over us as he had over my bike, leaving us crushed in the verge.

She shook me off and walked towards him. 'You're a beast. A filthy pervert. A liar. A murderer. We'll get you.'

He turned away, got into his car and started the engine. Charley stood kicking it, pounding the boot with her fists. He would drive over her. He only had to reverse and she'd be under his wheels. I ran to her but before I could reach her the car moved. It jerked forward and then stopped.

'Go home, Charlotte! Your poor mother's got enough to put up with without you being silly. Go on, just go home and behave in a sensible way.' And he drove off, squealing his tyres on the tarmac.

'The smug bastard!' she said.

'He could have killed us,' I said. 'When he thinks about what you said he may come back. We've got to get help. We're not safe on these quiet roads.'

She didn't seem to be in a state to go anywhere. She just sat on the verge and cried. I stood over her feeling helpless. I should have sat down and cuddled her, comforted her. After what she'd accused that man of she might have thought I had foul motives as well. It was too embarrassing. I just stood, pathetically useless, while she cried. It's not easy, being male.

14
Charley

It's typical: hysterical female and strong silent male. Both useless. I don't think we could have played the scene with Short John worse if we'd tried. I don't know why I didn't have the sense just to be my normal sulky self. Now he's driving off knowing we're on to him. Stupid, stupid, stupid.

Simon's down on the ground as well, fiddling in his rucksack, not looking at me. He must be fed-up. And especially with me. He gets a map out and opens it. 'What are you doing?' I say, to break the tension.

'Looking for another way home,' he says, 'in case he comes back.'

I suddenly realize what he means. Short John's already killed once. He's shut Simon in a shed. He'll be desperate. A neat hit-and-run in the middle of nowhere. Just a tragic accident and a driver too cowardly to stop. We're cycling happily along, chatting. We hear a car behind. So what? There are always cars on roads. Then? A desperate realization as I fly through the air? Perhaps I'm not killed outright? Perhaps he drives off? Simon dead beside me, me in agony dying slowly before help comes.

I look at Simon and see the same terror in his face. We look down at the map to avoid each other's nightmare. His finger traces a route that takes us in a very roundabout way to the town. We will be safe in the town, surely?

Simon's mother isn't there.

There's a note: 'Gone to visit Dad'. The house feels very empty, besieged by invisible hatred. I see suitcases standing in the hall. Simon's very edgy. He told me why they had to be away for a while when we stopped for a rest. He talked about going first to his Gran and then on to his aunt. They'll go away again as soon as the trial starts, or as soon as there's any more publicity, moving round to avoid the papers. He doesn't like being alone in the house and I'm not much help. In the end we decide to go to my house, tell my mum. He's not keen, thinks she'll hate him too, but it's better than sitting doing nothing.

So we're back on our bikes and cycling through the streets, and get home. He's pretty reluctant to come in but I push him in front of me and close the front door behind me so he can't bolt for it. Which is a pity, because we walk into the kitchen and find Short John sitting at the table as usual with his cup of coffee.

'Hello, love,' says Mum. 'Who's this?'

This time I'm calm and sensible. No shouting and screaming. It's different in my own home. Mum drinking coffee with him, all peaceful, all normal. It's hard to believe the nightmares. It's hard to believe the truth. It looks as though it's one of her better days. She's more alert, more herself.

'Coffee, Simon?' I ask. He nods. 'Just a friend from school,' I tell Mum. I see Short John raise his eyebrows at me but he doesn't say anything. I make coffee for us and Mum gets Simon sitting down and asks him about school. Which he finds embarrassing because he doesn't really go to my school at all. Short John cottons on to this and seems to find it amusing. But Simon's a good liar and manages to keep going, especially as I interrupt him all the time, seeming bossy. We even manage a row about an imaginary geography teacher. It helps that Mum really isn't interested, isn't paying attention. In the past she'd have known straight away something was up.

I haven't just lost a father, I realize. I've lost a mother too.

There's an awkward pause while I'm thinking this. I suddenly realize Mum wants to talk to me but won't with Simon there, and we want to talk to her and won't with Short John there. I guess he's spun her some story about me cracking up and they're going to send me for therapy or something. It's a good plan: convince people I'm mad and no one will listen to anything I say.

'You've met Simon before, Uncle John,' I say suddenly. I don't know why. Perhaps I am mad. He looks at me, a curious expression on his face. He's puzzled. He can work out why I was keeping quiet about who Simon really was, and that probably suits him. It gives him the chance to make me look deceitful. I think I need to stop him doing that. I think I need to make something happen. I cannot cope in this world of shadows silently mouthing at me.

'You remember,' I say. 'When you locked him in that farm shed.'

'Charlotte . . . ' he begins, but I interrupt. The adrenalin's flowing now. I'm on my own territory, cornered, and I'm going to come out fighting. The fact I've always hated him helps.

'You remember,' I say. 'Those ruined farm buildings near where Dad died. You pushed him into a shed and locked the door and drove away and left him.' Simon's white-faced and useless next to me. Mum's staring at me as if I'm raving. At least she's actually paying real attention.

Short John pushes his chair back and stands up. I've rattled him and he doesn't know what to do. 'I'll look in tomorrow,' he says to Mum. 'We need to sort something out fairly urgently.' And he's gone.

I sit down, suddenly shaking.

'Do have a biscuit, Simon,' Mum says, all polite as if nothing unusual had happened and she pushes the tin across the table. Her manners work perfectly even when she's away in her land of grief. I can't leave well alone.

74

'He did,' I say. 'He locked him in and drove away. Didn't he?' Simon nods. He seems to be incapable of saying anything but his neck muscles still seem to work.

Mum looks at him. She can quite believe I'm barmy, gibbering, but Simon looks normal and respectable, the sort of boy mothers hope their daughters will bring home. 'Simon is Simon Lomond,' I say and I feel Mum instantly tense beside me. Suddenly he's not the right sort of boy at all. A murderer's son. My father's murderer's son.

'His father didn't do it. We know he didn't. We need you to tell the police what we've found out. They wouldn't believe us.' And then I tell Mum the whole story while Simon's neck muscles continue to prove they can still work whatever's happened to the rest of him. There's silence when I've finished.

'Not John,' Mum says. 'Not John. I can't believe that.'

'Why did he lock Simon in the shed?'

Mum shakes her head. 'He could have just been angry with Simon, wanted to teach him a lesson. He probably came back ten minutes later. It could be his land. I don't know.'

'What about the fake taxi?'

'That doesn't have to be anything to do with him.'

'It's a bit of a big coincidence,' I say but I lose heart. She's not prepared to listen to me. I feel a moment of remorse as I realize I've bounced her. I remember how I hated Simon when I first realized who he was, when I still believed it was his father who was the killer. Now just because I feel he's the only one who understands, he's the only one I can talk to, it doesn't mean that Mum has to feel the same instantly. She's not going to rush round to the police station as I expected.

'I'll talk to Mr Colworth when I see him next week,' she says, as if humouring a small child. Mr Colworth is Dad's lawyer, was Dad's lawyer, is Mum's. I haven't met him. Mum likes him, says he's very good, but I don't think he can be up to much if there's all this trouble with the business.

'Next week!'

I get up in disgust and beckon Simon to follow me. We go out into the back garden and sit under the apple tree and I say nothing. To be honest, I'm ashamed of Mum. She's been taken in totally by Short John, always has been. She likes people too much.

'He'll move the car,' Simon says suddenly. It's the first thing he's said for ages. It's a sort of I-told-you-so, but very politely put.

'He didn't move it after he locked you up.'

'Perhaps he thought I hadn't seen it. Perhaps that's why he shoved me in the shed. As soon as I got out I ran like mad and I've not been back since, so it worked. But he must be worried we'll convince someone eventually.'

'If he moves the car, we've no evidence at all,' I say.

'Yes we have!' Simon suddenly shouts. 'How stupid I've been! I took photos just before he grabbed me.'

'So where are they?'

He looks embarrassed. 'At the chemist's. Mum lent my camera to my cousin, the one we were staying with. They've gone to Cornwall and she'd lost her camera on a school trip so Mum told me to lend her mine as a sort of thank-you for putting us up. I took the film out and took it to be processed and then Mum suddenly said we were coming home and I forgot about them. I'll have to try to get them.'

'I've got a camera,' I say. 'We'll go back and take some more pictures and get them processed at a one hour place and then if no one listens we can send them to the police, anonymously.'

I sound braver than I feel. Going back gives me the horrors, especially now Short John knows we're on to him. But there's no alternative. I've got to do

something. Simon doesn't look too pleased either. 'I'll
meet you in the morning,' he says.

'Too late,' I say. 'If he moves it, he'll want to do it in
the dark. That means it'll be tonight. He won't risk it in
daylight.' It's then I get this terrible idea. 'We ought to
be there after dark. We can photo him driving it, with
flash. He'll be surprised and dazzled and we can make a
run for it up the hill. . . '

As soon as the words are out of my mouth I want
them back. They're too right to ignore, but much too
dangerous.

15
Simon

I knew that what we were doing was mad, dangerous, pointless. I could hear Mum's scolding voice in my head even before we started. The weather had been building up all day and was now at its most oppressive. We needed a storm to clear the air. We certainly needed to clear the air.

I had made Charley agree that we would leave notes on our beds saying where we had gone as a safety precaution. I said it wasn't fair just to disappear (perhaps for ever, I thought but didn't say) and that we'd be in enough trouble if we were found out and that leaving a note would help our case. She was worried her mum would look in on her and find it too soon and come screaming after us. I rather hoped she did, but didn't say.

We cycled through the dusk by our new route. By the time we reached the bridle path it was almost dark, that thick summer grey. There were flickers of sheet lightning and mild grumblings in the distance and the weight of the air pushed against us as we rode up the hill. We stood panting on the top, putting off the moment we would have to walk through the long black vegetation down to the farm.

A sudden stab of brightness forked down, lighting up the whole countryside. I counted automatically: ten. Charley yanked my arm and set off down the overgrown path. It was darker after the blinding lightning and the plants held my feet and tried to trip me. I wanted to take my torch out but was more afraid of watching eyes in the blackness below. I thought we must be making enough noise to alert anyone and tried to go quietly but that slowed me down and Charley merged into the darkness ahead. I ran a step to catch her up, tripped and fell.

Another great flash lit the world. I saw Charley standing, a black shape against the sudden brightness. The crash came after five this time and a fat drop of rain fell on my face. 'Come on!' she urged me.

We stumbled down the path. More lightning, louder, closer thunder, heavy drops of rain increasing. The ground was slippery and we ran and slid to the gap in the hedge. Our momentum carried us through and into the nearest building. Its black mouth swallowed us. We stood panting as solid water fell outside and banged on the corrugated-iron roof louder than the thunder. It was suddenly cold and I shivered in my wet clothes.

Charley was rummaging in her backpack. She took out a bar of chocolate and passed some over to me. She said something but I couldn't hear anything except the violence of the rain. She tugged my arm again and pointed. The lightning lit up the farmyard. The barn with the car hidden in it was the next along. She seemed to be saying we should go there. I shook my head. We would drown trying to get there, and be killed if we were found there. She pulled but I resisted until she let go. Next thing I knew was that she was running like a maniac through the falling water.

I cursed. I couldn't bear to be here on my own and I think she knew that. There was a lull in the rain and I took a great breath and ran. It was like struggling through an upright river. I ran into the barn and crashed into something hard and fell and rolled on the concrete floor. A flash lit the world and the whole building shook and resonated with the instantaneous blow of thunder. My head rang as if I'd been struck.

Charley seemed to go mad with the madness of the storm. She danced, shrieking, in the doorway, answering the storm with her own wildness. The lightning gave a moment of clarity, everything sharp-edged, and then the blackness shut down again, leaving a vivid after-image seared on my eyeballs.

In one of those black patches I saw the blur of headlights in the distance, approaching.

I grabbed Charley and held her still and pointed. In that brief moment the rain eased and the lights pointed straight at us: malevolent eyes of a beast stalking us through the land of darkness.

Charley screamed, more in triumph than terror. 'Got him! We've got him!'

We were at the heart of a storm, next to the most vital evidence in a murder, with the killer of her father approaching and, and . . . Charley was rejoicing!

The rain increased its fury again. I tugged at her. 'We've got to hide!'

In the next flash I saw her face, just centimetres from mine, lit from within by a wild excitement. 'In the car,' she shouted back and pulled me towards it. I was off-balance and stumbled after her. We banged into the car and I heard her fumbling for the door handle.

'No! No! The keys, the keys!' Nothing could be crazier than to hide in the car. I felt my way to the driver's door, opened it and took out the keys. White headlight beams shone past the entrance to the barn. In the next lightning flash I saw an old trailer in the corner and pushed Charley towards it. We crouched behind it as the headlights moved to and fro like a searchlight and then shone straight in.

Car doors slammed and two men were silhouetted black against the headlights. Two tall men. I heard Charley gasp and found her hand and held it tightly. Not Short John as she had expected, as I had expected. One 'friend' of her family was one thing; two strangers was something else. I crouched tight, hoping I was hidden, hardly daring to look, but having to.

The men walked between us and the car. One of them opened the door. 'Where are the keys? You said you left them in.'

The other man moved past him and bent forward. 'I did leave them. I know I did.'

'They're not here now.'

'I can see that. Someone's been. Kids perhaps.'

'If it's kids,' the first man said. A great crack of thunder interrupted him and he spoke again when it had grumbled to silence. 'If it's kids they may tell someone, if only their mates. Word may get round. We'd better torch it. It's not safe to move it.' I squeezed Charley's hand harder. We could have been in the car, if she'd had her way.

'We'd better move the car first,' the second man said. 'The whole place could go up.'

They walked back, black against the headlights' beam.

'We've got to get out of here,' I whispered in Charley's ear.

'Can you drive?'

'Yeah, Dad taught me. A bit, anyway.'

'We've got to get the car out.' I stared at her as their headlights moved back, and then away. 'It's the only evidence we've got,' she said. 'If they burn it, your dad's completely had it. Come on, we've got to go now. Come on!' and she tugged at me violently.

The keys were in my hand. The storm raged about us. I was totally terrified.

16
Charley

I'm totally terrified as I get into the car. Suppose it
won't start? Suppose Simon crashes it into something?
I slam the door and lock it. 'Lock your door!' I scream
at him. I don't know whether he does. He's fiddling
about, trying to get the keys in. It takes for ever and
I'm shaking but I stop myself saying anything
somehow.

There's a roar as the engine catches first time. 'Thank
you, God,' I say and then the car jerks forward and
Simon swears. 'Where's reverse? Where's reverse?'
Suddenly he's in reverse and we leap backwards and
into junk on the far side of the barn and the thunder
drowns the noise we're making. 'Lights!' he's screaming.
The car leaps forward with a high-pitched roar and the
lights come on and we're heading fast for the two men
who are on the road in front of us.

I slam my feet down on the floor and Simon must too
because the car goes faster and screams like a mad beast
and the men leap out of the way and we hit a gate-post
and crash off it into the opposite hedge and clang off
that into the side of their car and then we're juddering
down the farm track.

I look behind. I can't see anything. It's as though
we're in a diving bell below water: blackness and
wetness surround us. Our headlight beams pick out
falling water. Even the storm sounds further away, a
distant rumble. We're on our own.

But won't be for long. The men will be jumping into
their car, turning it round, driving expertly after us.
We're still screeching our way, inching our way, along
the track. We seem to be going nowhere, noisily.

'Change gear!' I shout. He ignores me. Perhaps he can't hear me over the engine noise.

I stare behind but can't see anything. Perhaps we damaged their door when we bounced off their car. Perhaps they're creeping after us with their lights off, following the little red eyes on the back of our car, waiting to pounce. If Simon tries to change gear and stalls . . .

Suddenly there's a hedge straight in front of us. I think for one panicky moment Simon's driven sideways and then realize we're at the road. 'Left!' I shout and he turns left. I don't know if he stopped to look but nothing hits us and we're still isolated in our underwater world.

Behind, and off to the left, I see light. Their car's headlights. They are after us. Simon's managed to change gear and the car's stopped screaming in agony and I calm down a fraction and start to think, sort of. What I'm actually doing is shouting at Simon.

'Faster! They're coming!'

'It's no good going faster,' he says, surprisingly calm. 'I can't drive faster than them. If I try, I'll crash.'

We come to the junction with the main road, the road Dad was killed on. I realize I have such a clear picture burnt into my mind that I know what to do.

'Turn your headlights off and go left. There's a gateway on the right soon. There! Stop! Put the lights off while I open the gate.'

Simon obeys like a robot. Luckily the gate opens easily. I wave frantically at Simon and he edges the car in. 'Left behind the hedge,' I whisper, stupidly trying not to be overheard. He stops and gets out and I shut the gate. He's shaking all over and leans against the car. I take his hand and lead him away further along the hedge.

Headlights. Tyres squealing on the corner. A car racing past us. I find I've been holding my breath and let it out. Then a car—the same car?—racing back.

'We beat them!' I say, and hug Simon.

'What are we going to do? We've got to get home. The car will be seen in daylight.'

'Put it back,' I say. Suddenly I'm brilliant. 'Where's the one place they won't look? Put it back in the barn, and cycle home, and sort everything out tomorrow.'

'Suppose they come back while we're driving?'

'Suppose nothing,' I say. 'Let's just do it now.' And I go and open the gate. I don't want him thinking about it and freezing up. I wave firmly at him and it seems to work because the car jerks backwards and then swings round. He drives through the gateway and I shut it and get back in the car. He's sitting staring ahead and gripping the steering-wheel.

'Turn left,' I say firmly, as if there's no alternative. I know, and I expect he does too, that we could just get out, grab our bikes, and cycle home. But that wouldn't be the end of it at all.

The car jerks forward into the darkness. 'Put the lights on!' I shout. He fiddles around and the wipers swish and then the road ahead is lit up. He manages the gears more smoothly this time and we are quickly, too quickly, back bumping down the farm track. This is the danger point. Have those men come back too? Can they see our lights from wherever they are, and will they creep down after us?

In my nervousness I fidget about, opening the glove compartment, fishing in the door pocket. There's nothing in either. The car's been cleaned out. It's probably fingerprint free as well, except for ours I suddenly realize, and start another panic. I feel under my seat and my fingers feel the edge of a piece of paper. I stretch further and pull it out. It's a page torn from a notebook. I can make out writing but it's too dark to read any of it so I stuff it into my pocket for later.

The headlights show an empty yard. Simon drives

carefully back into the barn, back where we started from and switches off the engine. He sits holding the wheel.

'Take the keys,' I say. They'll be some sort of evidence I suppose even if they do burn the car. He takes them out, slowly, so slowly, and I get out my side and go round and open his door. 'Come on,' I say, 'it's not healthy here.'

He stumbles as he gets out and I hold his arm and pull him towards the yard. We're not safe yet. I get him across the yard and up on to the path. This is now absolutely sodden after the storm and I'm quickly wet through above my knees and squelching in my trainers. This seems to revive Simon and he strides up the hill faster and faster. I struggle now to keep up with him as the plants catch at me and the branches of the hedge lean out to scratch.

'Wait!' I shout but he pays no attention, if anything goes even faster and it's all too much for me and I start crying with tiredness and frustration. It's a nightmare struggle in the wet and the dark, getting nowhere, and Simon moving further and further away. I want to curl up in a ditch and wait until I wake up but I keep my head down and plod on at my own pace.

And then I'm at the top and Simon's holding the bikes and waiting for me and I'm so relieved I just fall against him and cling on, crying. I realize he's embarrassed, standing stiffly, holding the bikes, not knowing what to say. I stand up, wipe my nose on my sleeve and say, 'Sorry. I'm all right now,' and take my bike from him.

'That's OK,' he says, and we free-wheel down the track to the main road.

Down the track and straight into Short John.

17
Simon

It was one fright too far. Dad arrested. Followed in the street. Car chase in a thunderstorm. Now free-wheeling down a hill in the dark to run straight into the man I had been hiding from—it wasn't real. This was all a nightmare, a practical joke, an April fool. No one could believe this or take it seriously. No one. I couldn't.

I overtook Charley, braked, rested my feet on the ground, and laughed. This annoyed him and he started shouting at me, which just made me laugh even more.

He took two steps towards me, grabbed my handle-bars, and shook then fiercely. 'Just shut up!' he yelled right in my face. I did, suddenly absolutely terrified. He kept hold of the handlebars and leant past me. His voice dropped, slow, emphatic:

'Charlotte, what do you think you're doing? Your mother is out of her mind with worry. Don't you think she's got enough to trouble her without you going out in the middle of the night, and with the son of your father's murderer?'

His words dropped in the stillness of the night like a lightning flash. They lit up the desolate landscape that surrounded us: fathers dead or imprisoned, life withered. Everything else was nothing.

'At least you left her a note to say where you were,' he said. 'I'll take you home now. Lock your bike up and I'll bring you out for it in the morning; I'll bring my rack to put it on, save you cycling back.'

His breath brushed my ear as he spoke. His voice held me more securely than his hands on my bike. The soft black night isolated us.

'I'm not coming with you.'

I wanted to turn my head, to look at Charley to support her, but that man's face was so close to mine that I couldn't look back towards her.

'Don't be silly, there's a good girl,' he said, a bit sharper. 'You know me, you've known me all your life.'

'And hated you.'

He stepped back at that and I could turn and look over my shoulder at her. She had got off her bike and was holding it in front of her at arm's length, ready to drop it and run back up the hill. I got off and did the same. I didn't want to be left alone with that man.

'You've not still got that crazy idea about me being responsible? I thought you'd have got over that. Your father was my friend, for goodness' sake.'

'Why did you rub out the tyre marks? Why were you prowling round the farm? Why have you been following Simon? Why did you lock him in the shed?' The questions tumbled out of her as if they'd been jostling in her mouth, waiting to be asked. I stood there between them, not part of this private battle.

There was silence, a tense silence.

'You kids,' the man said, 'you think adults are perfect.'

Charley laughed at that. 'I think you're perfect?'

'That's not what I meant. I didn't mean good. I mean, you think adults always know what they're doing, act sensibly. We don't. It doesn't get any easier, you know, when you're grown up. I mean, you panic. You do things you know are silly, even while you're doing them, but you can't stop yourself.'

Was he saying he killed Charley's father? By mistake?

'It's been hell these last few weeks. I did some silly things; I couldn't cope. I know that. Look, I'll explain when I've got you home to your mother. I'll tell you both.'

'I'm not coming with you. Go and tell Mum I'm all right and I'm coming home. Simon will be with me. She's not to worry.'

'It'll be much quicker by car. And safer.'

'I'm not getting into your car,' she said. 'You go and we'll follow.'

'I'll ring her on the mobile. You speak to her and see what she says. She'll tell you to come back with me.'

'You ring her. Tell her I'm OK. Tell her I'm coming back with Simon. If you don't go now I'm going back up the hill and you won't know where I am.'

The man turned and got in his car and slammed the door and drove off and we cycled wearily back to Charley's house without speaking.

'Come round about eleven tomorrow,' she said. 'We'll talk to Mum.' She went into her house and I saw her mother coming towards her with her arms ready to hug her. I saw again how like her mum Charley was, except her mum had given up and Charley was fighting. I went home and got back into bed without my mum knowing I'd been out of the house. If she'd been waiting up for me I'd have told her everything, as we'd planned before, but next morning, sitting at breakfast, I couldn't face breaking into her brittle brightness and I pretended to go to school as usual. My life had become a mixture of total cowardice and incredible foolhardiness. I certainly can't believe what I, we, did next; it must have been someone else.

I was like a rabbit on the road in the dark. All my life up to now the headlights of my parents' care had been shining on me, keeping me frozen in my place. Suddenly the lights had been switched off and I was in the dark. No wonder I rushed about in wild circles.

I lurked about until just before eleven and then went round to Charley's house. She must have been waiting for me in the garden because she came furtively out almost as soon as I turned the corner.

'We're going round to his house,' she said. I stared at her. 'He's just arrived but he doesn't know where I am. He'll be safe here for a bit. Come on!'

I followed her.

Looking back now I think that was the moment when our behaviour crossed from rather stupid to totally insane. I can't explain it. It terrifies me now, what we did. At the time, I just felt as if I was being carried along by a huge wave, thrown up on the beach spluttering and sprawling, and then sucked out again, out of my depth, out of control, over and over.

I followed her. She had her bike round the next corner and she led the way through the streets, concentrating as if tracing the path through a maze she almost knew by heart. She stopped at a house that looked like any other house and rang the bell.

'Hello, Aunty Margaret,' she said to the ordinary-looking woman who answered the door. 'Uncle John asked us to come round and get his notebook off his desk. He needs it for something he's arranging with Mum. This is my friend Simon.' She stepped forward to be kissed.

'Hello, dear, how are you? How's your mother? Hello, Simon, nice to meet you. Yes, let's have a look, dear. It's not like John to forget things. It's lucky you caught me; I'm just off out.'

'He's got a lot on his mind,' Charley said. 'I don't know what we'd do without him.' I stared at her. 'You must be busy. Uncle John told me exactly where it is. I won't be a moment. You chat to Simon, get him to tell you about his dog, you'd love it.' And she rushed past through a room at the back of the house leaving me standing in the hall with my mouth open. We don't have a dog. Mum hates them.

Fortunately Mrs Short John didn't want to talk about dogs, at least she didn't want me to talk about them. She wanted to cluck about Charley: how brave, how sad, that awful man, how could he? I suddenly realized she was talking about my dad, but she wasn't really. She was talking about a man in the papers, someone quite different, no one I knew.

Charley came back, tucking something into her pocket. 'Thanks, Aunty! Must rush! Bye! Come on, Simon,' and she pushed me out of the door.

As soon as we were round the first corner she stopped. 'We'll wait here until she goes out. I unfastened a window. As soon as she's out of sight we're going in.'

'Why?'

'To find the evidence, of course. Here she comes. Keep back and keep still!'

Insane, both of us.

18
Charley

Skirt John drives off in her little Fiat. I always call her that in my head, which is unfair as she's really quite harmless, unlike her poisonous husband. 'Come on,' I say and we cross the road and walk in their front gate, trying not to look furtive. I expect Simon to complain and bleat about danger and crime but he follows me like a little lamb.

I lead the way round the side of the house and stop halfway along. I pull Simon half into a lilac bush. The strong scent of its flowers seems to hide us. We're straight opposite the window of Short John's office. I look cautiously round, trying to spot prying eyes in neighbouring windows but the lilac screens them from me just as much as it screens me from them.

'Wait here!' I whisper, then realize there's no need to keep my voice down. 'Wait here,' I say in a normal voice and immediately feel less frightened. 'I'm going to open the window. Keep a look-out.'

There's a flower bed to cross first. I try not to step on any plants. I get my fingernails into the join and ease the window open. It swings silently. I reach over, grasp the far edge of the window sill and pull myself into the room. I stand quite still, listening. I can hear nothing. I lean out of the window and beckon to Simon. He inches over.

'Wouldn't it be better if I stay out here and keep watch?' he says. I think about this. I can see he's scared—I'm scared—and doesn't want to come into the house. It might be a good idea to keep a look out. But if anyone sees him lurking about in the garden they'll be very suspicious. The Johns haven't got any children, and anyway he ought to be in school. Like me.

'Come in out of sight,' I say firmly and reach out to help him climb in. We're standing immediately next to Short John's desk, next to the chair. I sit down, suddenly weak in the legs. Light comes through the window over my right shoulder in the approved way. Everything in the right way, that's Short John. Or light would come in if Simon wasn't standing blocking it. 'Get out of the light,' I say and he moves to stand behind me.

It's a tidy desk. Telephone, answering machine/fax, computer and printer, pen holder, page-a-day diary. I'm just about to try the drawers when I suddenly stop. The diary. I have a confused memory of a diary page. I pull the book towards me and open it where the ribbon marker is. A list of bookings. Just like Dad used to keep. Tears sting my eyes and I turn back the pages, trying to clarify the memory that's worrying at me. I rush past the day Dad was killed and suddenly see it.

A jagged edge. A page has been torn out. And I know where that page is. I put my hand into my jeans pocket and take out the piece of paper I had found under the seat of the fake taxi last night. I unfold it; smooth it out. A page from a diary. Slowly I put it down on the book. It matches, of course: date, ragged edge, handwriting— two handwritings. The neat bookings taken over the phone by Skirt John. A scrawl in Short John's ostentatiously macho style:

WEDNESDAY 7 MAY

8.30 Davey 13 Fairfield Close: station

9.15 Corben 53 Stoneham St: Thorney

11.00 Hall 39 Deanfield Av: station

11.33 Heapy from station

TAKE NO BOOKINGS IN PM TODAY

10.30 Thorney, towards Grafton

'Got him!' I say. 'We've got him.'

The light darkens. Simon's moved back between me and the window. 'Move away from the window!' I say sharply.

'It's my window.'

Short John. Standing right outside the window. Looking at me fitting the page back into the diary.

'What are you doing?' he asks, all pleasant.

'Aunty Margaret,' I say, desperately thinking.

'Yes?'

'She's just gone out. She'll be back soon. She asked me to help her with the dusting.' It sounds stupid as I say it. Where is my duster? What's Simon doing here? I close the diary and push it to the edge of the desk furthest from the window.

'I see,' he says. 'I wonder why she put the alarm on when she went out?'

'Alarm?' I repeat stupidly. 'We didn't hear an alarm.' Giving myself away.

'Not one of those noisy things that just annoy the neighbours,' he says and holds up his mobile phone. 'Our alarm just rings me up and I come round and have a quiet look and find my office window wide open and you sitting at my desk and your suspicious friend as well and I'm expected to believe you're doing *dusting*?'

I sit. There's nothing to say.

'Don't think about running off,' he says. 'I know where you live, as they say. I'll come round and switch the alarm off and we'll have a little chat. OK?'

I get my voice back. 'We'll come out,' I say. I really don't fancy being in the house with him. With a killer.

He stares at me for a bit. 'Fair enough. I don't want to crowd you. But I'd rather you didn't climb out of the window and scuff the paint. I've only just decorated in there. Go out of the back door and sit on the bench in the garden. I'll come in the front, switch the alarm off. Make us all a nice cup of coffee and come and join you.'

'Right,' I say. I don't really have any choice. He stares at me again and then turns and walks away. Simon lets his breath out in a long sigh. I open the diary again and take out the torn page. I hand it to Simon. 'Put it in your pocket,' I say. 'If there's any trouble, you run for it. Let's go and have this nice coffee he's making us. Let's hope there's no weed-killer in it.'

The coffee tastes perfectly normal, but then I don't know what weed-killer tastes like. I've passed the point of caring. Simon and I sit side by side on his garden bench and Short John sits on a deckchair facing us. It's really not the best thing he could have chosen, as he seems to realize. It's designed to lie back in looking relaxed.

'Truth time,' he says.

'You first,' I say, and shut my mouth firmly.

'I didn't kill your father, Charlotte,' he says. 'Believe me. But I was used in the plot. And Simon's father was involved in it too, that's for sure.'

'Used?' I say.

To my horror he collapses into tears, sits hunched up in his stupid striped deckchair and cries. I feel sick.

When he starts speaking it's difficult to make out what he's saying; it's broken sentences with a chorus of sobs and sniffs. In the end he calms down and becomes quite clear. I make him say it twice more, mainly because I just can't believe it. Then he says, 'Wait here!' and goes off into the house.

'Do you believe him?' Simon says.

'I don't know,' I say. 'I really don't know.'

We sit there for a few minutes and then Short John comes out. 'I wrote this last night,' he says. 'I've printed out a copy for you. I am so terribly sorry for what's happened. I feel so guilty, but I don't want to go to the police, to stand trial, to go to prison. I think I'd kill myself first.'

'What about Simon's dad?' I ask the jelly.

'I'm sorry,' he repeats in that silly way. 'If he's involved, he'll be in trouble. If he isn't, he'll be cleared.'

'Like all those other innocents who spend fourteen years in prison?' I say.

'You do what you think best,' he says, and goes back into the house.

We sit with the sheet of paper between us and read it. It's what Short John told us, but clearer. I don't know how Simon feels. It certainly can't be comfortable for him. It's not comfortable reading for me. I find I'm instinctively edging further away. This sheet of paper is pushing us apart.

MY INVOLVEMENT IN THE EVENTS OF MAY 7TH

I was rung on my mobile on the morning of
Wednesday 7th May. I don't know who rang me.
The man was very threatening. He detailed
several incidents recently in which I had been
seriously inconvenienced—false call-outs,
two flat tyres, petrol drained from my tank—
things I had put down to persecution by
mindless teenagers. He said these were just
'mild warnings'. He said my taxi could be set
fire to. He said my wife might find some
'unpleasant things happening to her'. I
assumed he wanted money but he said that he
just wanted a small job done. I was to collect a
taxi from the disused farm buildings off the
B375, leaving my own car there, and drive to
Thorney at 10.30 that evening and 'draw
attention to myself'—'squeal around a lot,
bang doors, hoot, rev the engine outside some
houses'—and at 10.40 set off fast towards
Grafton. I was then to take the second left
which would bring me back to the B375. I was to
leave the car exactly where I found it and
drive home 'and keep your mouth shut, or else'.

When I got to the barn and found the car
waiting for me I saw that it was crudely
disguised as one of Tony Lomond's. I thought
this was a bit of persecution of another taxi
firm: the police would be round to
investigate and cause him a lot of grief. I
should have rung them, but I had no idea who
these people were and I took their threats
seriously. I didn't think what I was doing
would cause Tony any serious harm. He could
well have a good alibi anyway.

96

So I did exactly as I had been told except I skidded a bit too much and hit a lamp-post and dented the rear door. That caused several curtains to twitch. I was so worked up that I missed the turn and did a violent three-pointer in the middle of the road and then calmed down a bit. I put the car back and came home, hoping that would be the end of it but knowing in my heart that these people would be back.

I got a terrible shock when I heard that Bill Westcot had been killed and realized that I had played a part in it. Again, I know I should have gone to the police, but I had no evidence. Then I heard that Tony Lomond had been arrested and I assumed that he was involved, either slightly, like me, or at the heart of it.

I just had to go and check things. I knew it was a silly thing to do but in the end I couldn't keep away. I passed a kid on a bike that I now know was Tony's son and shouted at him because I didn't want him seeing me at the place where it happened. After my first visit I kept going back. I found some tyre marks I'd made turning round and tried to rub them out. I followed the kid one morning for no reason— I was just cracking up, I guess. I went to the barn one day and saw the kid there again and panicked and shut him in a shed. I calmed down later and went back but he'd got out.

All this is just my word. I have no evidence.

19
Simon

When I read Short John's 'confession' as I suppose
you'd call it I was totally depressed. Dad had to be
innocent. Therefore someone else was guilty. That
someone had been Short John. Now that it looked as
if Short John wasn't, suspicion pointed straight back at
Dad. Who else was there?

Charley looked at me, puzzled, worried, desperately
unhappy. Her father was still dead. There was no doubt
about that. She had trusted me, as a friend. The son of
her father's murderer could not be a friend, or be
trusted. Just the suspicion would be enough. The least
suspicion.

'Do you think this is true?' she asked.

I could have said, no. I could have said it was all lies
from first word to last. I think that was what she wanted
me to say. I couldn't. At this moment, sitting on the
bench in what had been the enemy's garden I had to
say: 'It sounds true. It fits.'

'What about your dad? Did he do it?'

She asked as if making conversation at the end of part
one of some TV serial in which the obvious suspect has
just been arrested. I made myself look at her. 'No. No,
he didn't.'

There was a pause, an awkward silence. Then she
burst out: 'Who are the two men who came to the barn
last night to burn the car? Who rang Short John up? It
can't have been your dad; he'd have recognized his
voice.' She went on staring at me. Then she reached out
and took my hand. 'I don't think your dad was
involved.'

'Why?'

'I don't know.' Then she took her hand away and looked away and said, 'I suppose because I like you too much to believe it.'

We sat in silence. That was a great comfort, the only real comfort I had had since this whole long arctic night had started. A great warm duvet, but not a dawn. The blackness still stretched for ever.

'Belief's not the point,' I said.

'Right,' Charley said, standing up. 'Let's go prove it. Where can we go and talk without flapping ears?'

'The public library,' I said, remembering it as a refuge from the icy blasts before. She seemed to have forgotten completely about going and telling one of our mothers what we knew. She had moved, I realized later when I thought about these strange and terrible weeks, into a fantasy world. I would not have been surprised to see her step into the phone box we passed and turn herself into Superwoman, except the box was one without a door, so it wouldn't have worked anyway. But she had succeeded in spreading her cloak over me and carrying me off with her. If I'd looked down I would have crashed but I carefully kept my eyes shut in the warmth of her darkness. She was no longer moving through the real world in which what you did was guided by common sense and rules, and in which adults were there to solve problems.

'Hello again,' the librarian smiled. 'How's the project going?'

Fortunately I remembered my lies. 'Fine, thanks. We need a bit more information though.' She smiled again, and held out two pencils and a wodge of computer print-out.

I led the way to the local history shelf and took out a couple of books at random and carried them to my usual table. Charley took one of the sheets of paper. She wrote with exaggerated care:

Possible events

1. false trail laid by SJ to incriminate S's dad

'How did that work?' she asked. 'I mean, why go to all that trouble?'

'That's why the police arrested Dad. He was seen by lots of witnesses behaving strangely in Grafton just before the time of the . . . the . . . '

'Pretty thin evidence,' Charley said, and hope leapt in me as I realized for the first time that it wasn't much at all. I had never believed Dad had done it, but I'd always assumed the police must have a very strong case against him. Charley wrote again:

2. S's dad follows with fare soon after
3. Dad collects a 'fare' in Grafton and drives towards Thorney. Fare stops him on a quiet bit of road and he is KILLED

'Perhaps it was an accident,' I said. 'I mean, they just meant it as a warning but something went wrong.' She looked at me and then nodded slowly. She crossed out 'killed' and went on:

3. Dad collects a 'fare' in Grafton and drives towards Thorney. Fare stops him on a quiet bit of road and he is KILLED attacked as a warning—
Plan to get 3 taxi firms in one go:
—make SJ do something he'll have to keep quiet about
—beat Dad up
—make S's dad suspiciously close to both incidents
THEN
burn fake taxi to look like joy riders
make anonymous phone call to police!!

'That's why they came for Dad,' I said. 'A tip-off.'

3 firms out of business.
RESULT: MAJOR TAKE-OVER

'But it went wrong,' I said.

'The bastards! He loved his business. It would have broken his heart to lose it. They're still getting away with it. Mum'll sell out to Short John and then they'll get him and your dad will be in prison . . . '

'Are you all right, dear?' the librarian asked.

'Hay fever,' Charley said through her tears. The librarian produced a box of tissues from under her magic counter and brought them over. I put a clean sheet of paper on top of Charley's notes.

' "Vernacular Rural Architecture", that's an interesting project. And "Canals of the East Midlands". Great!'

I opened the book nearest to me. A picture of a barn stared up at me. I wrote HAY BARNS on the paper and started to copy the drawing, feeling stupid like you do in school when a teacher has caught you out but isn't saying anything.

'Thanks,' Charley said, and blew her nose. That seemed to be the signal for the librarian to go back to her computer. Charley took the piece of paper I'd been drawing on.

What we've got
the fake taxi
SJ's confession and diary page

It was a short list, and we couldn't be sure we still had the taxi. Then Charley tapped my heading. 'Move those straw bales,' she said. 'Hide the car behind them. If the car goes, we've had it.'

Action Plan
1. *hide car*
2. *photographs*
3. *collect more evidence*
4. *set trap*

I added 'what?' to 3 and 4 on the Action Plan and we went to buy a snack for lunch.

20
Charley

I go home and there's Short John in our kitchen,
talking to Mum. When she turns her back to fill the
kettle, her bent back, her back bent under the
enormous invisible sorrow that she's carrying around,
he scribbles on a piece of paper and pushes it over: 'I
MUST talk to you.'

'Uncle John,' I say, 'come and look at the garden.' It's
feeble but it's the best I can do. He follows me out of the
back door and we walk slowly down the lawn pretending
to admire Dad's neat beds. There is something terrible
about the flowers he planted blooming on when he's not
here to see them.

'I've been threatened again. Rung up.' Good, I think.
I hope they make you sweat. 'The car's gone. The one
disguised as Tony Lomond's taxi. It was driven off.
They went round to destroy the evidence. It was dark
and there was that storm and suddenly someone drove it
at them, and away. They think it was me. They want the
car back.'

I don't say anything.

'Do you know anything about it, Charlotte? These are
desperate men.'

If he'd said 'Charley' I'd tell him. 'Do you think I'd
drive cars round in the middle of the night? I can't
drive, remember. I wouldn't let Dad teach me when he
wanted to.'

'You were there. You and that boy. Come on, I saw
you. Did he drive the car?'

'You'll have to ask him,' I say.

Mum taps on the window and holds up a mug to show
my tea's ready. I wave and start back towards the house.

103

He catches hold of my arm and I shake him off irritably. I'm not having him touching me.

'I've got to be at the old farm tomorrow morning at eleven. They're coming then. Get hold of that boy and meet me there as soon after ten as you can.'

'Go to the police,' I say. 'I'm not going near that place again. I've spent too much time there already.'

'There's no evidence. There's just my story. Please. Just get the boy to meet me. If not at the farm, somewhere else. But I've got to have something to tell them. Please. Look, I'm on your side.' And we go back into the kitchen and I take my mug of tea up to my room and lie on my bed and stare at the ceiling. Then I go and ring Simon.

Amy comes round in the evening, which was kind of her because I'm not much fun at the moment. Most people keep away from you when something awful has happened, as if it was catching. Mum excuses them, says they're embarrassed. I think they're selfish. I'm desperate to see normal people, to have my mind taken off what's happened for a bit. Grief's hard work; you need a break from it sometimes. People are shocked if you smile. I think they'd faint if they saw me laughing, like I do with Amy this evening. She tells me how Miss Corben caught Kylie copying Emma's homework and how Kylie tried to convince her that really Emma was copying hers. It was a nothing story really but Amy acted it all out and made a great drama of it. She's great. She seems to know when I just want to talk about Dad and get tearful and when I need to laugh.

She knows Mum doesn't know I'm not going to school and puts on an act for me when she leaves. Mum kisses her; she's not shocked that I've been laughing. 'Don't forget I want to be early tomorrow!' she calls as she gets to the gate, as we arranged, and waves. She leaves a glow behind her in the emptiness of the house. I carefully pack my school bag with the things I've agreed

with Simon and then watch TV with Mum. Neither of
us enjoy it, but what else is there in the evening? And
Mum's trying now. Sometimes there's someone there.

Next morning's bright and sunny again. 'You'd think
this was some wonderful place,' Simon says, 'the way we
keep going there. Day after day after day. I've lost count
now how many times it is. Each time it's worse, isn't it?'

I grunt and then we have to cycle in a single line
because of the traffic and I distract myself by making up
a holiday brochure for the farm:

MURDER THEME PARK!

Thrills for All!
Be a murderer or be a victim
or be the Great Detective—
it's *your* choice!
Come to Blood Farm for an exciting day. You will be
kidnapped, locked in a shed with a carrier bag on your
head, drive a car through a thunderstorm . . .

The trouble is, too many people would want to come. I
add a line, a front cover perhaps:

Calling all ghouls and vultures: see people suffer!

We cycle along the too-familiar road: Simon's quite
right. I've picked some of Dad's flowers and they sit all
bright in my basket, mocking. Simon watches as I lay
them on the verge and then we hide our bikes behind
the hedge and walk up the hill. We reckon it's safer this
way.

'Have you seen your dad?' I ask, suddenly remembering
my criticisms of other people yesterday evening and
realizing how selfish I'd been. OK, my dad's dead but

his is in prison. And yes, he did want to talk, how he wanted to talk. It all spilled out. He'd had no one and had bottled it all up until he must have been ready to burst, except that's what males do—bottle it up, I mean.

His mum goes every day. Apparently you can if he's on remand. Simon's only been twice. The first time he wanted to go and the second his mum made him and he hopes she won't make him go again. It's not that he doesn't want to see his dad, but it's not his dad. He's not in prison clothes or anything, that's something else about being on remand, but you have to go through all the locked doors and security checks, and you have to leave him behind when you come home. That's the really hard bit, the bit he can't cope with.

So we sit on top of the hill in the sunshine. I seem to have done nothing these last dreary days but cycle to and from this hill. I suppose it's filled the emptiness of the days, the restless need to do something, anything, and the restless inability to stick to anything I start. And there's something detached about this hill top. You might almost think we'd stepped through some wardrobe into a different world. To my left is where Dad was killed. Below is where we have just hidden a car used somehow in his death. Further away are Mum, and school, and the empty future. Reluctantly, very reluctantly, we have to go down into that future.

The farm looks peaceful from the hill top, like a model farm. We walk down the hill towards it. We've walked the long grass down now and there's a clear path: our bit for the countryside. With such trivial thoughts I keep my mind off what we are doing: walking—yet again!—into that farmyard where dangerous, desperate men are due. But the sun is shining, Simon's with me: nothing nasty seems quite believable. And Dad's dead so I really don't care: nothing worse can happen, nothing my whole life long.

I almost enjoy moving the car. Bright sunshine
changes things. Moving the straw bales is something
else. They are heavy, scratchy, obstinate. It takes two of
us to shift them, and then we have to shift them back.
We pile them up just inside the doorway so it sort of
looks as if the whole barn is full of them. There's plenty
of space behind, a secret hide-out Simon says. I'm not
sure I like the sound of that.

It looks quite convincing from the outside. There's a
way to scramble over the bales at one side. We shift
some around to make a platform to stand on and move
some of the top layer to make a couple of gaps we can
see through and a gap to photograph through. I take the
microphone of Dad's miniature tape recorder and put it
between two bales at about head height. I hope it will
catch enough conversation. I push the lead through and
Simon tugs it the rest of the way.

We are hot and sweaty and scratched, but ready. We
have nothing left to do but wait: always the hardest
thing to do. I sit back on our platform and rub my back
against the straw. The physical itch is easy to deal with.
We wait. And wait.

21
Simon

At last we heard a car coming. I looked at my watch: nearly ten. It should be Short John. Charley stood up and peered through her spy-hole and I looked through mine. That familiar black BMW stopped very neatly immediately opposite us. Then it started up again and I thought he was going to drive away, but he just turned round, ready for a quick exit in case of trouble perhaps.

He got out of his car and stood there, looking around. 'Charlotte!' he called. 'Hello?' Then he leant into the car and blipped his horn. He walked up and down like someone anxious for their bus.

'Sweat, you swine,' Charley muttered.

He went out of sight. I remembered visiting a castle in Wales. The towers had arrow-slits pointing in all directions so that the defenders could see what was happening. I had forgotten that lesson. We could see straight ahead, and only straight ahead. All the action might well take place off stage, certainly off camera. It was too late to do anything about it now.

He came back and rested his hands on the top of his car. His head went forward until it was touching his hands. His shoulders started shaking.

'He's crying again,' Charley said, awed.

Then she climbed over the top of the bales and walked across towards him. He didn't hear her at first but then his head came slowly up and he stared at her. Sunlight glinted on the tears on his cheeks.

'You're really in trouble, aren't you?' Charley said.

'I kept telling you. You wouldn't believe me.'

I watched Charley, wondering what she was going to

do. She didn't seem to know herself. She stood facing Short John with his car between them. She looked tensed, ready to run. If he really was telling the truth . . .

'Where's the car?' he said.

'How would I know?' she answered. For a moment I thought she was lying, saying she didn't know, and then I realized it wasn't exactly a lie, more an evasion. She seemed to be testing him, still unwilling to believe him as she disliked him so much. I wondered if she had some reason she hadn't told me about; he didn't seem that bad to me.

'The car went. You were there. And that boy. Is he here now?'

Again, she didn't answer him directly. 'We need evidence. We need to tell the police who's responsible.'

He looked at his watch and started round the car towards her. She backed away and he stopped. 'They'll be here any minute. They're dangerous. They want that car and people will get hurt if they don't get it.'

'Who are "they"?'

'I don't know. I keep telling you, I don't know. What I do know is you're behaving very strangely. I'm a friend of your mum's; I was a friend of your dad's. Margaret and I are in serious danger. Can I say it any more simply?'

'If I knew where the car was,' Charley said, 'if I did, what's it worth to you? What would you do for me?'

'Are you asking for money?'

'I want help. I need to know who killed Dad. I need to know why. And I want to get Simon's father out of prison.' Thanks, I thought. I didn't think I'd be able to stand there negotiating with the enemy like she was. I suddenly realized that, since that morning the police had come and arrested Dad I'd been running and hiding: not able to face anyone. Not able to face my own feelings either.

I stood up and leant over the straw bales. 'We need

evidence,' I said, facing him head on, coolly. A small step for a man, I thought, but a giant leap for me.

'Hiding in the dark,' Short John sneered. 'Letting a girl do the talking.'

'That's pretty sexist,' Charley said.

'There just isn't time for this,' he said. 'I don't know how to get evidence. All I know is they'll be here and there'll be serious trouble.'

'I'll tell you how to get evidence,' I said, and I did. I don't know why adults don't watch TV properly. It's full of useful information.

'Do that properly and we might remember where the car is,' Charley said.

She walked away from him without waiting for an answer. There didn't seem much he could say. Then we heard the sound of a car coming down the farm track and she scrambled over the bales and dropped down next to me. She took the camera out of the bag and poked it into the gap she'd made and then fiddled with the zoom lens. I fidgeted with the controls of the tape recorder. It was up to Short John now, I knew, but if we made a mess of it we'd be no better off. And could we trust him?

The car, one of those four-wheel drives that Dad always calls Sainsbury's shopping trolleys because that's all most people use them for, came into the yard and stopped, almost touching the front of the BMW. I heard Charley click her shutter and the auto-wind going. It sounded very loud in the silence. My finger hesitated on the on button. Nothing happened in the yard for minutes. I could see a man through the open window but it was no one I recognized, no one I had seen before. Short John had come round the back of his car and was standing about halfway between it and the barn we were in, as we'd told him. Could we trust him?

I looked quickly round. There was no other way out.

If he betrayed us, we'd be cornered. They'd have us, and the car. Everything we had been through would have been for nothing. The drive through the storm in the dark. I could have had a nasty accident in that car . . . I could still have a nasty accident. Charley and I could be accidented in the car . . . They seemed good at arranging accidents.

I switched the tape recorder on. It was no good expecting the worst all the time. One of us ought to be able to escape at least. All the years you spend playing dodging games when you're little ought to be some use.

The man leant out of his window. 'Where's the car?' I heard the click-whirr of the camera.

'I told you, I don't know.'

The man opened the door of his shopping trolley and got out. He was smartly dressed: suit, tie, shiny shoes. Another man got out of the other side: jeans, T-shirt, trainers. I didn't know either of them. They could well have been the men from last night. Equally, they might well not have been. I really didn't want to know any of them. The stage was set: three men, two shiny cars, and a decrepit farmyard.

'Now then, Johnny,' Suit said, 'let's not go on with this. We don't have time. Just tell us, where have you put that car? We know you were here. We saw that nice shiny BMW of yours. This one, with the broken windscreen.' While he was saying this Trainers picked up a lump of concrete from the ground and then stepped forward and smashed it down once, twice, three times: windscreen, headlamp, headlamp. The broken glass caught the sun and sparkled.

'Nice paint on these cars,' Trainers said, and stood with his lump of concrete poised over the bonnet.

Short John took two steps backwards, closer to us. 'Carry on,' he said. 'It's insured. Malicious attack by vandals is covered in my policy.'

'Are you covered?' Trainers asked, and hurled the concrete. It crashed to the ground where Short John had been standing before he'd leapt aside.

'Is your wife insured?' Suit said quietly.

'My wife?' Short John said.

'Darling Margaret,' Trainers sneered. 'Got her covered, have we? Get her written off and get a newer model with the money, will we?'

'I don't know where the car is, and that's the truth. It's no good threatening me. I just do not know.'

'Trouble is,' Suit said, calmly, smoothly, 'can we believe you?'

'Why would I want to hide it from you?'

'That's a very good point,' Suit said, 'a very good point. Why would you? Trouble is, we don't really have the time just now for guessing games. Our employer really wants that car, wants it, sort of, now. Now, as in yesterday. Not now as in after some guessing game.'

'Do you think Darling Margaret might know?' Trainers asked.

Short John looked over his shoulder at the barn we were hiding in.

He had been doing well up till then. If the tape and the photos were OK we'd got vital evidence. He should have done something, told them a lie about where the car was, got them away long enough for us to go to the police. Should, should—easy enough afterwards to say should. He was under pressure. His body behaved instinctively.

He looked over his shoulder at the barn we were hiding in. That was enough for the men. They turned and looked at each other and smiled.

'Perhaps we won't need to bother Margaret after all,' Suit said, pleasantly. 'I expect she's a busy woman. Do you know what I fancy? I just fancy a cigarette. Trouble is, I'm a very careless smoker. The number of times I've dropped a burning match and even a cigarette end that's still glowing. Shocking. Number of fires careless smokers cause. Talk about insurance.'

He took a packet of cigarettes out of his pocket.

22
Charley

'I should get your car out of the yard,' the passenger says to Short John. 'Unless, of course, you want vandals to write it off for you.'

Short John steps towards his car. The passenger steps towards his. They're like western gunfighters slowly, delicately watching each other.

That's right, I think. You all move your cars and we can get out and make a run for it.

Then the driver steps forward. The other two freeze.

'Do you think that's a good idea?' the driver asks. 'Are we sure he's going to be sensible and just go home to Darling Margaret? We don't want any busybody calling the fire brigade, do we?' The argument goes on and I suddenly wake up to reality.

Fire brigade! My mind must be on holiday. They're going to set fire to the straw bales, which will set fire to the old wooden barn, which will set fire to the car, which will explode, and . . . Somewhere in all this they'll have the added bonus, though they don't know it, of setting fire to us.

What are we doing here? What am I doing here? What has happened to my life? Questions fill my mind but are pushed out by that great bully, my imagination.

Nightmare takes over. Smoke fills my mouth, choking me, heat blisters my skin, bubbles my flesh, tigers of wrath roar in my ears and . . .

> # TRAGIC LOSS OF TWO LIVES
> # STRICKEN FAMILIES MOURN
>
> Yesterday the remains of two young people were found in the old barn that burnt down. Their blackened skeletons, lying next to the shattered bits of a totally unrecognizable car, were identified from dental records. They were holding melted plastic lumps which are believed to have once been a camera and a tape recorder though it's now impossible to say for sure. Police are working on two theories. One is that they had been smoking and carelessly caused their own deaths. The other is a suicide pact because of the tragic way their families have been linked together . . .

I try desperately to regain control of my mind. We have to get out. We have to get out with our evidence. We have to get out and away. If we climb over the bales, even through our carefully constructed gap—fire exit!— they will see us and we'll be caught and that will be the end of it. Back to bodies in the barn.

I am frozen with terror. So brave I am, in theory. So brave I am when there's no real danger. But now my imagination already feels the jagged lump of concrete smashing my head, already feels my limp body chucked over the bales, already feels the tongues of the flames nibbling at my flesh.

I reach out my hand and grasp Simon's. He's shaking all over. We have had it. Run and get chucked back. Stay. We're going to burn whatever we do.

'We've got to go in different directions,' Simon says through his chattering teeth. He says it twice before I make out what he's saying. Somehow, just talking as if it wasn't all over helps. 'If one of us can get away they won't dare hurt the other.' This is the best thing I've heard for years. There's suddenly a little hope.

'We must take the camera and the recording,' I say.

'I'll just take the tape,' he says. 'It'll go into my pocket. If they see me holding the recorder they may guess what's been going on. And I'll be able to move better.'

I can see he thinks he'll be the one to get away— typical male arrogance. I'll show him. I rewind the film and take it out of the camera. It's an awkward lump in my jeans' pocket but he's right: I feel a lot freer without the camera in my hands.

The argument seems to have ended and Short John walks to his car. He gets in, starts the engine, revs it a bit and then backs away from the four-by-four. The rat, I think, going to save his own skin, leave us here. I always knew that was what he was like, under all the smarm.

He reverses the car violently back towards us and I think for a moment he's going to hit the bales. Then he brakes suddenly and gets out of the car, leaving the engine running.

'There's flaming glass everywhere!' he shouts. He picks up a bit of wood from the ground and brushes away at his seat. Then he walks round to the other side, opens the passenger door and brushes away there. He opens the back door, leans in, and then comes round behind the car and opens the last door. All the doors are now wide open and the engine's running.

'It's OK, I'm getting ready to go,' he calls. I know, and Simon seems to know at the same moment, what he's doing. I can't believe it, but it seems to be true. I never thought he'd do something like this.

The two men are shouting at him, telling him to get a move on, stop fussing about his housework. He walks over to them leaving the car. 'Have you looked behind that barn?' he says. 'It looks like tracks going round behind.' I guess he thought they'd rush off and have a look and he could drive away with us hidden in the back of his car.

They're obviously suspicious, I can see, and suspect there's a trick, though they don't know what it is. So, they're not falling for that old one. The passenger takes him by the arm and says, 'Show us then, Johnny,' and they all walk out of sight. Now is when we have to move.

We scramble through the straw bales and drop down to the yard. We have seconds only; they'll be back. I can hear their voices behind the barn.

'You run up the hill,' Simon says. 'I'll drive out.'

I look at him. I know he's right: divide up and we've a better chance. But I can see me panting and slipping up that path and that violent man effortlessly chasing me and grabbing my leg and pulling me down and finding the film and losing his temper and I leap into the back of Short John's car as Simon gets into the front and there's no time to argue as he puts it into gear and we screech across the yard.

The wide-open doors catch on the gateposts at the entrance and the doors slam and mine swings open again and I nearly fall out trying to close it. I turn and see the men running for their car and Short John with his fist in the air in a victory salute.

It's a repeat of our last mad drive except it's broad daylight and bright sunshine and Simon seems more confident and changes gear twice. The car stops screaming and bumps even faster along the track.

My exhilaration fades as we reach the road and Simon shouts: 'Which way? Which way?' There is no way to go. There's no future in this mad drive. At night, in a storm, you can get away with it: the whole world's mad and no one notices if you are too. But Simon can't drive a car in bright daylight along roads full of traffic. Either we'll have an accident and someone will get killed or we'll be spotted and the police will be after us . . . Just now that would be the best possible thing to happen.

I glance behind me and see the four-by-four coming up fast behind. 'Go left!' I scream and Simon stalls the car and the black monster fills the back window and smashes into us and I'm half-thrown, half-scramble into the front of the car. Simon bounces off the steering wheel and the impact jump-starts us and we're on the road with an oncoming car swerving to avoid us and blaring its horn.

There's another bash from behind that jerks us forward. I reach over to pull Simon's seat belt round him but he shouts, 'No, we're going to have to get out and run for it,' but I ignore him and click it in. If we crash, when we crash, he's not going to run far with a smashed-in head. I keep my hand on the button though so that I can release him instantly.

'Where are we going? Where are we going?' Simon is sobbing. The rush of air through the broken windscreen whips the words away and makes it difficult to think.

'To people!' I say as we reach the junction. 'Turn right! To people! The more witnesses the safer we are.' The more danger to them, I think, but don't say it. Two cars, one driven by a kid—'joy-rider' the papers would say—and one by a maniac, careering into a busy street . . .

There's more traffic on this road and Simon's under pressure. They're close behind, terrifyingly close, but they don't bump us again. Too many other vehicles, I guess. Then we're going up the hill towards Grafton and the car's complaining and Simon decides to change down before the bend and as we lose that little bit of speed there's another of those heart-stopping crashes as the four-by-four rams us and Simon loses control and we're straight across the road and into the hedge opposite.

The engine cuts out. My fingers release Simon's seat belt and we climb out of the car. Its front half is through the hedge blocking the way to the road. The enemy have pulled up a few metres further along and are running towards us. A lorry and a car have also stopped and their drivers are coming towards us as well.

'Run for it!' I say, and we turn and stumble up the field. Shouts follow us but we don't look round.

23
Simon

It was one of those nightmares: one horror after another. The only good thing was that they came so quickly that I didn't have time to panic. It was afterwards that was worst: thinking all the what-ifs.

For now, all my mind could cope with was forcing my increasingly reluctant legs up the field, instinctively trying to dodge the clumps of thistles and splodges of cow pat, scraping enough air into my chest, just keeping going.

I started to drop behind Charley. I desperately wanted to drop to the long grass, to lie and pant and to let what must happen happen. We could never get away. What was the point of going on? Then Charley reached her hand out and held mine and tugged and I somehow found a little more determination and staggered on. The field became steeper and then we were across it and at the other side.

The gate! We had just assumed there would be a gate. There wasn't. We went to and fro. There was no gate on this side of the field. A very well-kept hedge stretched all round the field, except for the one gateway on to the main road. A hedge of prickly hawthorn: impossible to climb over, to push through, to crawl under. It was the sort of hedge that had surrounded Sleeping Beauty: in the story it was covered with the decaying bodies of those who had tried to force their way through. I could feel its thorns scratching my eyes just looking at it. It was impossible, except that two men were walking up the field towards us. They had no need to hurry. There was nowhere we could go.

We could dodge. There was a whole field to play in. There was no way they could catch both of us. Two of them might catch one of us if they worked together, if they knew how to win the game. Which one would they choose? There were enough people watching down on the road for us not to be in real danger surely. Could we make them go for one of us, while the other took all the evidence?

Charley seemed to read my mind as we stood there desperately gasping for breath. She took the film out of her pocket and looked at it. The men were about halfway up the field, walking slowly but purposefully, a few metres apart. 'I'll throw it over the hedge,' she said. 'Give me the tape. I'll throw them together. You distract their attention so they don't see me.'

It made sense. It was the least worst option. I passed her the mini tape cassette. 'On three,' I said. I counted and then sprinted off to my left, watching the two men. They turned instinctively and started after me and then Suit said something and Trainers turned back towards Charley. I turned too and walked the way I had come, out of breath again. She smiled faintly at me and showed me her empty hands.

The men stopped about twenty metres from us. 'What's up, kids?' Suit said. 'You know something we need to know. You were hiding in that barn. Why?'

So they hadn't found the car. They didn't know about the camera and the tape recorder. There was something else they didn't know.

I nudged Charley and nodded my head towards Grafton. A flashing blue light was coming along the road at speed.

'We panicked,' she said. 'You were talking about burning the barn. We had to get out. He just left the car there. It was too good a chance. Easiest joy-riding we've ever done.'

'What were you doing there?'

'Someone said a car was there last week. We went to have a look. There wasn't anything. Wasted journey.' The blue light was closer, much closer. 'You frightened us,' Charley said. 'And then you bumped us off the road. We were frightened . . . ' She went on talking, saying anything, without making much sense. I was staring down towards the road.

The police car drew up across the gateway. Two policemen got out and started talking to the spectators. They pointed at us. The policemen moved to the gateway. One was talking into his radio. They stood there. Charley faltered into silence. Suit smiled an unpleasant smile. 'Let's all just go and take a look, shall we?' They didn't try to grab us. They just waited, thinking they had us cornered and we'd meekly walk into their open cage.

'OK,' Charley said. 'We can all go,' and she pointed down towards the road. The men turned and looked and swore. Charley laughed, a hysterical triumphant laugh, a laugh that said it was all over and we were safe.

'Come on,' Suit said, 'let's go and meet them together. We'll let you hand us over.' He muttered something to Trainers, who didn't seem happy, and they walked a few paces away from each other. Suit bowed and waved us through, mocking us it seemed. Charley laughed and strutted through the gap past them.

'Now!' Suit shouted. They leapt forward and grabbed Charley before we knew what was happening. They each held an arm and stood back from her as she struggled and kicked and screamed. The two policemen started running up the field. I ran towards Suit and tried to kick his legs. I had the idea of knocking him off balance but he just swung his arm and his hand caught me round the side of my head and I sprawled on the grass.

'Just stop there!' he shouted and everyone was suddenly still. I looked up and saw the knife in his hand and felt cold, thinking what might have happened

122

to me, what might be going to happen to Charley, of the scarlet blood on the green grass.

'I'm sure none of us want her hurt. Just back off before I do something you might regret.' The policemen took a step back. They looked puzzled. They must have thought we were the criminals and the two men were just public-spirited citizens. They hadn't been prepared for this.

'That's not very sensible,' one of them said. 'I don't know what's going on here, but you're putting yourself in the wrong like that. Just drop the knife and we can sort it all out. If that's your car these kids have taken and wrecked, let us sort it out.'

I expected Charley to shout out something, to explain, to accuse but she was silent. I sat on the grass, my head still ringing, trying to wipe cow pat off my hand without anyone noticing.

'It's not that simple,' Suit said. 'I haven't got time to explain now.'

'We can't let you take the girl,' the other policeman said. 'You must know that.'

Suit moved the knife over and held it to Charley's face. 'Don't think I wouldn't hurt her,' he said. Charley cried out and I saw a drop of blood like a red tear run down her cheek. He swung his arm out and held it so that the knife shone in the sun. 'You don't have any options,' he said. 'I'll tell you what to do and you'll do it.'

He will too, I thought. If they've killed once they'll do it again. The policemen don't know that. They probably think it's a case of road rage and he'll calm down in a minute.

'This is what you'll do,' Suit said. 'You'll walk down to the road. You'll get all those spectators away from here. You'll get in your car and drive away out of sight. Once we're away we'll leave the girl by the road. That's the deal. Take it, or take the consequences.'

'Give us two minutes,' the first policeman said and turned towards the other one.

'Drop your radios!' Suit said sharply. 'Now!' and his hand moved the knife back towards Charley.

The policemen put their radios down on the grass carefully. He stretched his arm out again. He seemed to enjoy tormenting them, making the most of the knife. Charley was standing frozen with terror between the two men, a red smear on her cheek. The two policemen were whispering to each other. Everyone seemed to have forgotten me, pathetic on the grass.

The policemen straightened up. They seemed to have reached a decision. I had too. Suit's arm was stretched out above me. The knife gleamed. I leapt.

24
Charley

Confusion describes it best. Confusion on confusion, and then more confusion. I think I'm now past all that confusion. I hope so. There should have been enough time since those terrible weeks. 'Keep looking forward,' Uncle John keeps saying. I know he's right but it's not always easy. The past hides in unexpected places and ambushes me when I least expect it. It needs dragging out into the open, but it's hard.

Like, if they show rugby on the TV now I have to leave the room. Somehow, seeing all those men piling on top of each other brings it all back: Simon's amazingly brave act, so unlike him it was. I hope I would have done it if it had been all the other way round, we like to think we're brave, but he had trailed after me all those awful days like a real wimp. I think that was how I put up with him then: he was such an inoffensive, pathetic, broken person. I felt stronger just by being alongside him: what had happened to me was far worse than what had happened to him but I was coping oh so much better. I had led the way, decided everything. Then— whoosh! Superman to the rescue!

I wish I'd actually seen it, been able to stand outside the scene and watch. However hard I try now it's still just a sudden confusion. One moment I was standing there in full sunlight held achingly tight by those two thugs while the policemen dithered and the next moment I was on the grass, face down, with a squirming, struggling mass of men on top—expecting steel slicing into me through the darkness at every moment. Then there was shouting and yelling and more police, and more. That was all one vast confusion. It was

125

later that I learned that Simon had leapt for the man's arm and taken him by surprise and the policemen had reacted almost instantaneously. I don't know what would have happened otherwise.

I've tried to talk about it since but Mum won't. She says I'm being morbid. 'He did, thank goodness,' she says. 'It does no good to brood on what didn't happen. He's a good boy. I'm glad you're friends.' And she won't say more. Uncle John keeps on about how he wishes he'd been there, he'd have sorted them out—without ever saying how. Then he takes the opportunity to say once again how brilliant he was, reversing the car to where we were, opening the doors, leaving the engine running, distracting the men, watching them drive off and then calling the police on his mobile. He makes a great story out of it and somehow the pleasure he gets out of it has taken away the fear I felt at the time. He's so pleased with himself. But I have to admit, he was brilliant.

Simon says there would have been one of those long sieges you see on TV sometimes: police unrolling telephone lines, mobile HQs, camera teams. In the end the men would have broken and let me go. 'I couldn't wait that long,' he says. 'I needed the loo. I had to do something.' Not just incredibly brave, but modest too. Making a joke of it all has been the best way to drive the past back, back to where it belongs, in the past. Making a good story of it all helps to sort out the confusion.

There was more confusion as we were taken away in police cars and had to wait until our mums came and then confusion through the hours of questions and more hours of waiting. I didn't have to go back to the barn or the field fortunately. I still haven't gone back. I will, soon. I've told Simon I want him to come with me: to where Dad was killed, to the barn, to that field. Soon, but not quite yet. They asked me if I would go and show them where I had thrown the tape and the film but

I said no. At least, that's what I thought I said. Mum now tells me I 'made my feelings plain' and laughs. It's about the first time she's laughed so I don't mind. She won't tell me exactly what I did say or do and I don't remember.

Simon did go with them and they found the tape and the film, and they rescued the camera and the tape recorder I'd taken from Dad's desk. And they found the car behind the straw bales. Gradually our story made sense to them, but questions, questions, questions. Over and over the same things until I was so confused that I started to make mistakes, to muddle things up. Somehow, they were happier when I did that. Mum says it showed it wasn't some story I'd made up—I still don't understand.

At last, eventually, it all began to make sense and it turned out that Uncle John had been right all along. He told the police exactly what he had done: that night in Grafton, thinking Simon's dad was involved and following Simon, muddling evidence. He was quite shaken by his interviews. It took him days to recover. The police didn't take any action against him but I think they were quite tough with him. He's got to give evidence in the trial, when it happens. The law seems so terribly slow. We'd really like the whole thing over and finished. Though it never will be over and finished as Dad will never come back.

We don't know if we'll have to give evidence, Simon and me. That's one last bit of confusion that's still lurking. The two men are apparently quite keen to shift the blame on to their employer. They're saying Dad's death was an accident, that they just meant to frighten him. If they end up pleading guilty the police say we probably won't have to give evidence. In a sort of way, we were the ones who caught them but no one's praising us. Simon's death-defying leap gets lots of admiration but otherwise we're just told off: stupid risks, missing school . . .

When the news came out Kylie came smarming up to Amy and me, wanting to be friends. I told her I'd had enough of bullies to last me a long time and she slunk off. I know who my friends are. Now I do. You can be so wrong.

'Look forward,' Uncle John says. He's partly right, I think, but only partly. The past is where we've come from, where we've left in store so much we care for. I don't want to forget the good bits, I don't want to forget Dad. It's no good taking one of those holiday brochure photos that cuts out the ugliness. That's how life is: mixed through and through. If you push the past away it goes into hiding and waits to ambush you. Face the dark and it lightens.

Other Oxford fiction

It's My Life
Michael Harrison
ISBN 0 19 275042 9

I knew something was wrong as soon as I stepped into the hall. The trouble was, I didn't know how I knew. If there had been obvious signs—anything unusual, any sound, anything at all—I would have turned round and walked straight out again.

But Martin doesn't walk out again and within minutes he finds himself in the middle of a nightmare. He is kidnapped and held captive on a canal boat—but that is only the beginning. When Martin finds out who his kidnapper is, and who he is in league with, the horror deepens and Martin has to use all his ingenuity to escape—with Hannah's help.

'The pace is fast, with plenty of action . . . '
The School Librarian

'Seriously recommended for anyone interested in the dynamics of kidnapping.'
The Times

Sea Dance
Will Gatti
ISBN 0 19 275090 9

In my dreams the hands were reaching out of the water to pull me down, down into the dark; that's what I always felt.

Willie Cormack hates the sea. He sees it in his nightmares, the raging ocean full of the ghosts of drowned fishermen, beckoning to him. But Willie lives on a peninsula on the west coast of Ireland and the sea is all around him. The only way to make a living is from the sea, and Willie is afraid of his future.

And then a lone sailor is shipwrecked on the coast in a storm and the tiny community is thrown into turmoil by the stranger who is so suddenly thrust among them. In the atmosphere of bigotry and suspicion that follows, a terrible tragedy seems inevitable unless Willie can meet his own fears face to face and pit himself against the very elements that haunt his dreams.

The Stones are Hatching
Geraldine McCaughrean
ISBN 0 19 275091 7

'You are the one,' he said. 'You must go. You must stop the Worm waking. You must save us.'

Phelim was the only one, they said, the only one who could save the world from the Hatchlings of the Stoor Worm. The Stoor Worm, who had been asleep for aeons, was beginning to waken. The dreadful sounds of war had roused it, and now its Hatchlings were abroad, terrorizing the people who had forgotten all about them, forgotten all the ancient magics.

But how could Phelim, who was only a boy, after all, save the world from all these dreadful monsters? And where could he find the Maiden, the Fool, and the Horse who were supposed to help him? As Phelim leaves his home and sets out on his quest, the words ring in his ears: 'You are the one. To stop the Worm waking. To do what must be done.'

The Night After Tomorrow
Sue Welford
ISBN 0 19 275108 5

January . . . the wolf month . . . wolf-monath . . .

Jess felt she had been broken to pieces. Nothing worked for
her any more. So it was good to get away and find some space
with her aunt in the country.

But the country wasn't quite as peaceful as she thought it
would be. In the forest there were strange noises and
movements. When Jess was in bed, there was the sense of
someone or something outside, watching, waiting for her. On
the farms, the cattle and sheep were being slaughtered by a
savage creature—the forest beast they called it.

And then there was Luc, who seemed to belong to the wild,
with his hypnotic amber-coloured eyes and long hair. Why
was he so interested in the forest beast? Why had no one ever
seen his mother? And what was it that could only be done
the night after tomorrow?

The Scavenger's Tale
Rachel Anderson
ISBN 0 19 275022 4

The taller Monitor placed her hand on my shoulder.
* 'You can't,' I squealed. 'My family's opted out.'*
* 'Nobody opts out, pet. Every human being has the potential to offer the gift of life to another. Now take it easy. Just a little shot. A nice sedative.' She took the sterile wrapping off a syringe-pak while the other held me . . .*

It is 2015, after the great Conflagration, and London has become a tourist sight for people from all over the world, coming to visit the historic Heritage Centres. These are out of bounds to people like Bedford and his sister Dee who live in an Unapproved Temporary Dwelling and have to scavenge from skips and bins just to stay alive.

Bedford begins to notice something odd about the tourists: when they arrive in the city, they are desperately ill, but when they leave they seem to have been miraculously cured. And then the Dysfuncs start disappearing. It is only when a stranger appears, terribly injured, that Bedford begins to put two and two together . . .

Against the Day
Michael Cronin
ISBN 0 19 275039 9

It is 1940. The Nazis have invaded, and Britain is now part of the Third Reich. All over the country, German military authorities are taking control, led by the brutal Gestapo.

But slowly, surely, a resistance is building throughout the land. A secret network of people are plotting to overthrow the Nazis and win back their freedom, at any cost. Frank and Les, two schoolboys, never meant to get involved—but find themselves part of a dangerous undercover operation that can only end in bloodshed . . .

From: *It's My Life*

Tuesday 18 December 3.35 p.m.
Martin . . .

I knew something was wrong as soon as I stepped into the hall. The trouble was, I didn't know *how* I knew. If there had been obvious signs—anything unusual, any sound, anything at all—I would have turned round and walked straight out again. I stood in the hall, one hand still on the door handle, the door still open behind me. I looked round. Everything was in its right place, including me.

I had been in such trouble last night that I didn't dare not be in the right place. INSIDE THE HOUSE BY TWENTY-FIVE TO FOUR. Those were my instructions. School finished at 3.15. I was allowed five minutes to gather my belongings together and fifteen minutes to walk home. Mum had been so angry yesterday that she had gone straight out and walked to school to find out how long it took. I had to be in my house. I was not allowed to go to any of my friends' houses. I was certainly not allowed to go to the shops again. If she rang up—when she rang up—I had to be here to answer. Or else.

I had an exact time to get home. I had got home on time, early in fact because I had hung around talking, just to prove I didn't care, wasn't bothered. I had then been so worried I might be late, might not be in for the phone call, that I had run some of the way. Now I was here, panting slightly in the doorway, but on time. But this was just the start. I had an exact timetable for when I was back. It was stuck to the fridge door with a magnet in the shape of a chocolate bar. A chocolate bar! Anything else would have been better: chains for example. They would be more suitable for a prison-house.

I was the prisoner. I was also the prison warden. The prison was guarded by telephone, and by fear of the 'or else'.

So, 3.35 and I was standing inside the hall and something was wrong.

'Hello!' I called.

There was no answer. The silence began to get to me. That was one reason I had got into trouble yesterday. I really didn't like walking into the house when no one was there, especially at this time of year when it got dark early. But I couldn't say so, could I? Mum kept going on about how I was a big boy now, the man of the house. She kept going on about how hard she had to work to keep me, how little money my dad gave her. How could I stand there and say I was too frightened to walk into my own house, was frightened of the silence?

It wasn't even the silence. It was the nearly silence. If you stood in the hall, like I was standing at that moment, and listened, you heard noises. A lot of them came from the road outside but when you shut the door there were still little sounds. If you are in a house by yourself there are always little sounds all around you. Probably safe sounds. But how do you know? I had tracked them round the house until I knew each one. It was worse in winter because the heating going on and off made a whole lot of different noises. I had taught myself to recognize them so that I knew now exactly what happened. Sometimes I thought it was best to put the TV on to drown out all the little noises and sometimes I thought it was best to be able to hear if someone was creeping up on me. I didn't like stepping into the empty house. I didn't like being in the house by myself. I would have liked to have been able to go round to a friend's house, but I wasn't allowed. I wasn't really allowed friends. And today I had orders. Today I had a timetable. Today I was going to have to listen to the little sounds.

No TV today. It wasn't on my timetable. Next was 3.40: A DRINK AND A BISCUIT. I shut the front door, hung up my coat tidily and walked into the kitchen.

I checked the time on the clock on the cooker: 3.37 it said. I had three minutes still in hand. Perhaps I should use those minutes to check the list of instructions on the fridge. I wouldn't have time later:

MARTIN

3.35: Get home

3.40: drink and a biscuit

3.45: do your homework

4.15: tidy your room

4.30: peel 4 potatoes

That's my life, I thought bitterly.

I opened the fridge and took out a bottle of milk and poured myself a mug. As I put the bottle back in the fridge the motor came on; another of the regular noises, and one of the friendlier ones. I went to the cupboard and took out the biscuit tin. Mum had probably counted them this morning so I'd better just have one, as instructed. She had been in a foul mood at breakfast, complaining about me, about the state of my room, and about having a headache. I put my one biscuit in my mouth as the phone started to ring.

The phone starting to ring always makes me jump; there's no warning, just this sudden scream. It's worse than a baby: 'Pick me up! Pick me up!' it yells through the house. I'd been expecting this call, the Secret Police checking up on me, but it still made me jump. I hadn't really got time to jump. She'd probably timed how long it would take me to walk from the biscuit tin to the phone so I walked briskly to it.

I put the last piece of biscuit in my mouth so that she would hear that I had so far followed instructions to the letter and put my hand out to pick up the phone which was nagging away at me still.

A hand came down on mine and held it down on the phone.

Another hand came over my mouth at the same moment. The phone rang and rang, crying out for attention, crying out in what Mum must have thought was an empty house. Every muscle of mine seized up. I thought I had stopped breathing. I thought my heart had stopped beating.

I was looking down at this hand on top of mine. It looked black and shiny like something that has crawled out of a swamp but it wasn't slimy on my hand. It was warm, and smooth and, strangely, almost comforting, like having your hand held always is. All I could hear was the phone shrieking. All I could feel was the warm weight of the glove pressing my hand down. It was as if my hand was crying, crying, and this gloved hand was comforting it.

The phone stopped suddenly, in mid cry. The silence was huge and filled the hall. I tried to open my mouth to breathe, why did I need to open my mouth, my mouth full of soggy biscuit? I realized somehow for the first time that a glove was squeezing my mouth shut. I realized it must belong to the other hand because I could feel a body behind me. Now everything rushed at me suddenly. The hall leapt at me. Panic ran along every vein in my body. It clung to my hair and pulled it. It danced in my stomach. It roared in my ears. It leaked out of my eyes and trickled down my leg.

'It's all right,' a voice said quietly behind my ear. 'Just be still. Be quiet.'

The hand moved from the telephone. It reached out to the coats that hung up by the front door. It lifted up Mum's blue mac. It dropped it over my head so that the world suddenly disappeared. I was inside a stuffy black cave. The voice spoke again.

'If you scream I'll gag you, tie your mouth up. You won't like that.'

The glove moved cautiously away from my mouth. I took in a great gulp of the stuffy black air. The glove instantly clamped its shiny self round my mouth again. I could taste my own saliva, cold on the glove.

'Do you want to be gagged?'

I shook my head. The glove moved again. I breathed in slowly, cautiously, as if I was stealing the air.

'That's better,' the voice said. 'Do exactly what you're told and you won't be hurt. Now, we're going to walk into the kitchen, slowly.'

One hand gripped my shoulder, hard, holding the mac down on it. I could feel the tension of the cloth pulling on my head. It was pulled towards me so that I couldn't see past it down to my feet. The hand pushed firmly. I took small paces, feeling where I was going. I put my hand out to find the doorway but my arm was slapped down sharply. The hand on my shoulder gripped and pushed.

'Where's the string?' the voice said. The man could obviously see it was a kitchen where everything had its place. My mug of milk was the only thing not where it should be. And me. I shouldn't be in the kitchen. I should be doing homework in my room.

I tried to speak but my voice choked. The hand shook me. I cleared my throat. 'Second drawer down.'

I was pushed a bit further. Held still. I heard the drawer being opened.

'Scissors?'

'Top drawer.'

I heard that being opened. I was pushed further, to my left. I was turned round, pushed back. I could feel the chocolate-bar magnet pressing into my shoulder. My back was to the fridge door. Its motor was silent now.

'Hold out your left hand.'

I held it out. String was tied round my wrist. The knot was pulled tight with his fingers between the string and my wrist so that it wasn't too tight.

'Now your right.' I held out my right wrist. Today I had to obey orders. Today, people had decided to order me around, efficient, organized people.

The same piece of string went round that wrist. It was pulled until my hands were touching and then it was tied in the same careful way. The string was pulled, moving my hands like a reluctant dog. The mac wasn't being held round my face now and I could see straight down and could breathe more easily. The string was being tied round the fridge door handle.

The man tugged hard at the knots and grunted. My brain had begun to unfreeze now. I thought of all the things people did on TV to escape from these situations. 'Try anything and I'll smash you,' the man said, as if he could see into my head. I looked down and twisted my hands so that I could see what time it was. I needed to do something and it was all I could think of. I stared at my watch but it didn't make any sense to me.

'Right,' the man said, 'you stay there nice and quiet and you'll be all right.'

I heard him walk away from me to the kitchen door. There was a pause, as if he was watching me. I stood still and breathed as quietly as I could in case he thought I was drawing breath to scream. There wasn't any point in screaming. There was no one to hear and he probably really would smash me. Why shouldn't he? And I didn't feel like screaming. I felt like becoming really small and invisible.

I heard the creak of the third stair and I knew where he was. I listened hard and heard a door being opened quietly. I couldn't tell which it was but it was upstairs. Knowing where he was, knowing he wasn't watching me, knowing he wasn't about to smash me made me feel better. I leant forwards and tugged at the mac and felt it pull up over my head and then it fell with a rush to the floor. Light dazzled me.

I stood still and listened. There were faint noises from

upstairs, drawers being opened perhaps. I looked all round me, looked at Mum's tidy kitchen. It was not quite so tidy now: my mug, a ball of string, a pair of scissors—all out of place, and all out of reach. I was tied to the fridge door with about ten centimetres of string between me and the handle. I couldn't reach anything except my timetable which sat on the white fridge door and glared at me. It would soon be time for me to tidy my room. It would be worse now because it sounded as though the man was untidying everything upstairs.

I looked at the knots. The ones on my wrists were out of reach because of the way my hands had been tied. I could reach the ones on the fridge handle but it was pointless. I did try to untie them. I had felt him tugging at them when he tied them and they were biting into each other like the worst shoe-lace tangle. The fridge magnet was sensible safe plastic with a little round magnet stuck on to it. There was no way I could use it to saw through the string like they would in a film. I stood there helplessly.

Then I realized: fridge doors open. I opened it cautiously. It gave that little sucking noise as the rubber seal came away from the main body. It sounded very loud to me. I hoped he hadn't heard it up there. I pulled it open as wide as it would go. Mum would shout at me if she was here: letting all the cold air out. I was now by the work-surface that ran between the fridge and the sink. The scissors were by the sink, still out of reach. Think! I urged myself. I tried to remember all the films I'd seen on TV, all the ways of escaping when you're tied up. Then I realized again. My mind seemed to work in jumps at the moment.

There was no way that my hands could reach the scissors, but my feet could. I turned to face the work-surface and put my hands on it. I jumped myself up, sort of pivoting on my hands and turning on to my front, pressing down with my elbow as I landed to stop myself sliding off again. I lay on my stomach, hands stretched out towards the fridge door and eased my feet along, gently, so gently. I could see the scissors in my mind, I could see them clattering into the sink, I could see the man rushing in, grabbing them, sticking them into my defenceless back . . .

I lay very still for a moment, listening. There was no pounding on the stairs, just the occasional quiet noises of someone searching. I stretched out my feet, slowly, slowly.

My trainer touched the scissors. I pressed down with my toe, tried to pull them towards me. They wouldn't move the way I wanted. They tried to slip further away. It took me a moment to realize it was impossible. Lying on my stomach I couldn't move my foot towards me along the work-surface. My foot would only come towards me through the air. I slid my whole body along until my head was pushing against the wall. I took my trainer off the scissors and carefully slid back as far as I could but they were still out of reach of course, because I couldn't move my hands far from the fridge door. I lifted my head and looked down. Mum's mac was lying on the floor below the work-surface. If I flicked the scissors off they would land on the mac, should land on the mac. If I missed they would be out of my reach for good and the clatter would call the man. Risk it! I said to myself. Go on, I said to myself, risk it!

I flicked my foot sideways and felt the scissors jump off. I heard by the sound they made landing that they'd fallen on to cloth and not on to the kitchen tiles. I twisted over and slipped down silently so that I was standing on the floor again and pulled the mac towards me with my foot. I twisted it round until the scissors lay at my feet.

At my feet. Still at my feet! They were completely out of reach of my hands. I was no further forward. At each stage I had a brilliant idea but each brilliant idea just led me up a new dead end. The man would come down soon, see what I had done, and smash me. Perhaps he'd have to kill me because I'd see his face and would be able to describe him and pick him out in an identity parade. I began to panic. I'd be a dead end soon. The fridge motor started up again, sounding very loud. I pushed the door shut, dragging the mac after me.

I had to do something to stop the panic rising, rising; I had to do something, anything, rather than stand there getting more and more worked up. In desperation I pushed my right trainer off with my left foot. I pushed away at my sock, pushing it down my ankle. I stood on the toe and pulled. With a jerk, the sock came off. I wedged my big toe through one finger hole of the scissors and carefully lifted my foot, twisting my knee to bring my foot right up. My fingers closed round the blades. Yes!

I cut through the string that held me to the fridge and then cut the string between my hands. I slipped my foot back into my trainer and the scissors into my pocket and stood and thought. Back door? Front door? Think!

Back door: out into the garden, over the fence, no one at home either side. Who would be in down the road? How long would it be before he caught me scrambling over the fence? Grabbed my ankle and scraped me off the fence? Would I get as far as the fence? Key to put in the lock. No, key to take off its hook and put in the lock and turn. Bolt to slide back. Noise. Time.

Front door: out and away down the road, people . . . but across the hall. He could be coming down the stairs, could leap down and grab me and . . .

The phone rang. Its sudden hysterical cry making me jump and run towards it. Mum.

'Mum!' I shouted as I picked the phone up. 'Mum! Help! There's a man here. He tied me up. Quick!'

There was a voice on the phone, not Mum's voice. 'Janet,' it was saying, 'is that you, dear? What's going on? Who's that shouting? Don't say I've got a wrong number again. Oh, this phone!'

'Help me!' I yelled, but the phone just purred at me.

All this time there had been more sounds, banging, running, and now jumping down stairs. I had had my back turned while I was speaking, facing the phone, facing Mum, I thought, hiding from everything else. I put the phone down carefully, thinking it was important that Mum could ring and then I turned, just as the man lost his balance rushing down the stairs and fell forward on to his face, sliding the last two steps and sprawling by the front door.

Front door: blocked. Back door: too slow. Stairs: blocked. Help! Why wasn't my dad here to look after me? Then I remembered and ran across the hall, pulled open the door to the cupboard under the stairs, crammed myself in, squirmed half round again, pulled the door shut, and pushed the bolt in. I sat, panting, remembering.

Mum and Dad had had one of their biggest rows ever in front of me over that bolt. I'd been nagging Dad, on and on, wanting a tree-house. I don't remember now why it was so important for me to have a tree-house but I remember it was the only thing I thought about for weeks. I couldn't have one. We didn't have a proper tree in our garden but I was too young to realize this. I thought Dad could grow one, or plant one, or build a tree-house somewhere else. In the end he put a bolt on the inside of the cupboard door. 'That's an inside-a-tree-house,' he said. It was great in there when I was small, squeezing in behind the Hoover and all the stuff that fills cupboards to the far end where the stairs meet the floor and I could really imagine I was living inside a tree. It was the sort of brilliant thing Dad thought of. Mum really went for him. Not safe, she said. I'd lock myself in. The bolt would stick. On and on and on. Taking away all the pleasure I had had, all the pleasure I had shared with Dad. I never went in there again after that row, until now.

I couldn't see anything, but you could hear quite a lot in there. I heard the man swearing. He came across to the cupboard and pulled at the door, expecting it to open. He swore again, kicked it.

'Open this door,' he shouted. 'Open it, or I'll smash it in and you with it, you little . . .'

I squirmed away from the door, round the Hoover, but couldn't get very far. There was more junk in the cupboard now, and I was much bigger. He kicked the door a couple of times and then just stood there. I could hear him breathing through the wood. Then it went quiet.

I felt around me, feeling everything and trying to remember what was in the cupboard, what might be useful. I managed to get the scissors out of my pocket. They might make him hold back a bit. Very soon, though, there were more noises, scraping and a bump against the door.

'If you won't come out, you can stay in till I'm ready for you,' the man's voice came. 'You won't move that in a hurry.'

His feet went over my head up the stairs, thumping down as if they would break through at any moment and land on me: thump! Thump! There was the ghost of an echo sighing down the stairs. Then silence. In the silence the noise from outside seemed louder for a moment. Then silence, nothing. There was a little edge of light round the door, enough to see where it was but not enough to see anything. I was in the muffled dark. I needed the toilet.

As I sat there in the dark, desperate for what Mum insisted I call 'the loo', I began to panic about air. It seemed to me that it was running out. I tried to breathe slowly but found I was panting. Panic came out of the dark and attacked again. It wasn't so bad when I was moving, doing something, just planning something even, but I couldn't just sit. It was like playing hide-and-seek when you can't bear not to peep and see if they're coming to look for you. I think I was safe locked in, wedged in, but I didn't feel safe. I didn't know what the man was doing, where he was. Suppose he set fire to the house to destroy the evidence and the witness? I listened for the crackling of furniture, sniffed for the smoke that would sidle under the door, sneak down my throat in the dark, fill my lungs . . . Why didn't we have a smoke detector like all my friends?

I moved quietly back to the door. I slid the bolt, slowly, carefully, silently. He might be there, waiting, his trap set. There might be nothing wedging the door closed. I would heave at it and fall out, straight into his hands. I moved the bolt back again and sat listening. There was no sound of breathing on the other side of the door; there was no sound at all.

I eased the bolt. I very lightly pushed the door. It moved about a centimetre, stopped. Something was holding it. I put my mouth to the crack and gulped at the air outside. I pushed a little harder. Nothing happened. I put the scissors down and turned round so that my back was to the door, wedged my feet against the Hoover, and pushed. There was a scraping sound as the door moved another centimetre or two, then stopped. The noise frightened me and I held on to the door, ready to pull it shut again. Nothing.

I knelt up and eased the door open. My fingers just edged through the gap. I bent them round and felt with my finger-tips. Soft: cloth: a chair. I felt down and felt the smooth wooden leg of the chair Mum always sat in to watch TV. I ought to be able to push that. But if I pushed it, it would make that scraping noise, it might topple over, crash on to the floor. The man would run down the stairs again, run more carefully this time. I must plan exactly what to do.

I shut my eyes and pictured the hall. Pictured where the chair would be when the door was open enough for me to slip out. Pictured the lock on the front door—that was my only escape route in the time I would have. Planned out every step in my head.

I wedged my feet against the Hoover again and put my shoulder to the door. I took a deep breath and pushed as hard as I could. Nothing happened for a moment and then it all happened at once. Whatever was holding the chair in place suddenly gave way. The chair slid across the floor. The door swung open and I fell forward on to my hands like one of those sprinters you see on TV.

Tuesday: 3.55 approximately
Martin

A hand held my ankle. I tried to get up but the hand jerked my leg and I fell over again. The voice said, 'I keep telling you: do what you're told and you won't get hurt. Do you think I want to hurt you? Don't make me, just don't make me hurt you.' The hand let go of my ankle and grasped my arm. I was pulled to my feet and pushed back into the kitchen. Mum would not be pleased. Her mac was lying on the floor with some bits of string. Two drawers were open. There was a dirty sock. There was a mug half full of milk. There was me. There was the man.

He pushed me back towards the fridge. He bent down and picked up Mum's mac and dropped it back over my head so that the world disappeared again. Somehow I didn't feel frightened now. I knew what was going to happen. He was going to tie me to the fridge again and take the scissors away. I would have to stay there until Mum came home. I could manage that.

It shouldn't be too long now, about an hour. I could manage an hour.

'I'm going to tell you what we're going to do,' the voice came. 'Just listen and if you do exactly what I say, you'll be fine and it will all end happily ever after. We've got two things to do. First, we are going to leave a message for your mother so that she knows what's going on. I'm going to sit you at the table so that you can write and you'll write what I tell you.'

While he was saying this he pushed me quite gently until I could feel my knees against the side of a chair. He turned me and I sat down. He pulled the coat forward so that I could see the table. He pushed a piece of paper in front of me and then a pencil. I recognized them. They had been in my room, waiting for me to do my homework. I knew the pencil well. It had been sharpened until about half was left. It had my tooth marks pitting the yellow paint so that it was flaking off at the end. It lay there now on the piece of paper, like a traitor. I didn't want to pick it up.

'Pick up the pencil,' the voice said, 'and write this.' Slowly I picked it up. Its feel in my hand brought back the safety of my room, the safe boredom of homework, of the sound of Mum downstairs getting supper ready. A tear dropped on to the piece of paper, spread out. Another followed. I sniffed, blinked, tried to hold it in. Boys don't cry, do they? I made myself remember how much I hated being made to stay in my room by myself between school and supper. Cosy family life wasn't something I'd had much of lately. Why cry, then?

'Write this: "Dear . . ." and then put whatever you call her. OK? "I am all right. I am not hurt. I have been kidnapped"—two p's—"and you will receive more instructions later. Do not"—underline not—"tell the police, or else." Now sign it.'

I wrote 'Martin'.

A hand in its glove came under the mac and picked up

the paper. I held on to the pencil and then slipped it into my pocket. I could feel it pressing against my leg, a comforting pressure. The man spoke again.

'We'll leave this on the fridge door where she'll see it. Now, this is the tricky bit. I've got to get you out of here without anyone noticing. It's up to you. You co-operate and you won't get hurt and we can get all this sorted out very quickly and you'll be home and safe and it will all be over. That's one choice. The other choice you have is to try to get away or attract attention. You might succeed. You might get away. If you do, I might too. And I'd come after you again. You'd never feel safe, would you? Any time you opened a door, I might be behind it. Any corner you go round, I might be waiting. That's if you're lucky and get away. If you're unlucky and don't get away . . . well, I'm going to get pretty annoyed, aren't I? I'm not going to be able to trust you. You might get seriously hurt and you'd definitely have a pretty uncomfortable time. It's a bit of a lottery, isn't it? And I don't think you've got much chance of winning.'

'I'll be quiet,' I said.

'You'd have to say that. I don't know whether you're telling me the truth or not so I'll not be able to trust you. Just remember that.'

I felt the mac being pulled off my head. Light didn't flood in as it had before. It was already getting dark outside. The man was standing behind me. I didn't turn my head to look at him. It would be best to let him think I wasn't going to try to escape, and then it could be easy to slip away in the dark. I'd need to get a good look at him so that I could tell the police. But I'd wait, pretend.

'I'm going to tie a piece of string round your wrist so that I can hold the other end. We're going to walk out, shutting the door carefully behind us. We will walk along the road and down to the canal. If you see anyone you know you'll smile nicely at them but say nothing and keep walking. Remember: your best bet is to do exactly what you're told.'

He lifted my left arm and put it on the table. He tied a loop of string round my wrist, just as he had before. Being tied up again made me feel how hopeless it was to try to escape. Everything I'd done, all the panic and all the feeling of outwitting him, had come to exactly nothing. Perhaps he was right. How could I beat a ruthless adult who had planned this all out? But why kidnap me? Why?

He finished tying the string round my wrist and gave it a tug to make sure it wouldn't slip over my hand. 'Get your coat,' he said.

I walked to the front door, to where I had hung my coat when I came in from school, so long ago it seemed now. I put it on facing the wall and then slowly turned. I don't know quite what I expected to see, some sort of monster I suppose. What I did see surprised me, it was so normal. He was just a man in the kitchen doorway, about the same height as most people, at least I couldn't say he was especially tall or especially short. He had a dark grey coat on, with the collar turned up and a scarf round his neck, rather pulled up round his face, and one of those flat caps, pulled down at the front. There wasn't much of his face showing through all this: a nose stuck out but that looked normal too.

He took one step towards me and bent down and picked up a blue bag from the bottom of the stairs. It was my bag. It was the one I used when I went to stay with Dad for the weekend. Why couldn't Dad be here to sort everything out? Seeing the bag made it all much worse somehow. It was bad enough that he'd come to burgle our house, but to take my bag! He should have brought his own bag to put the valuables in, but he'd have been disappointed in our house; there weren't any valuables. Perhaps that was why he was kidnapping me. I remembered something we'd done in history at school.

Morton's Fork, it was called. In the old days the tax collectors came round and looked at your house. If you looked rich they charged you lots of tax. If you looked poor, they said you must have been hiding your money instead of spending it and still charged you a lot of tax. He was in for a disappointment if he thought all our money was in the bank. We didn't have any money, as Mum kept telling me.

He carried the bag over to me and put it on the floor. 'Kneel down,' he said. I hesitated, not sure what he meant. 'Kneel down,' he said again, sharply this time. 'Come on, you've got to do exactly what you're told, remember?'

I knelt down next to the bag. He took the string that was hanging from my wrist and tied it firmly round the handle of the bag so that my hand was held level with it.

'Right,' he said. 'You hold that handle and I'll hold this handle. It'll look as if we're carrying a heavy bag between us, see?' His voice sounded as if he was pleased with himself, pleased at his cleverness. I held the handle next to me and we both stood up. He held the bag and the bag held me. It was very light, surprisingly light, as if it didn't have much in, but it looked full. He put his other hand on the door catch.

'Remember what I said. We walk down the street, nice and easy. Anyone you know, smile but say nothing. I'll talk if talking's necessary.'

He hesitated, almost as if he was nervous. I had another sudden thought. He probably was nervous. He was in danger, like me, but his was the danger of being caught, being put in prison.

'Right,' he said, 'let's go.' He opened the door and we went out awkwardly, sideways with the bag between us. 'Shut the door behind you,' he said. I pulled it shut. The catch clicked. The street outside had become dark and the street lights had come on so that there were pools of gloom between them. I looked for his get-away car or van but the only ones parked were the usual ones belonging to people in the road. We turned left and walked along. I wanted to ask him where we were going but I didn't dare. It was worse, not knowing, just walking away from home, walking into the darkness.